An Honest Mistake

by Henry Demarest

For my father, Marc, who taught me who I was

and for Nicole, who taught me who I wasn't

CHAPTER 1

I felt like throwing up. My stomach turned and my mouth became dry and as the dizziness set in, all I wanted to do was crawl under a rock and die.

It didn't surprise me, really, that it had come to this. Some part of me always knew it would end up this way. You can't escape destiny and ours was to be here, in this familiar place, together and alone at the same time.

I turned to look at her, for what I feared would be the last time. She was lying in the bed, her back to me and completely silent, except for the slick sobbing and labored gasps for breath every alternate beat. She clutched a pillow to her chest, gripping it tightly like she used to hold me, not wanting to ever let go. I envied that pillow for a moment, truly I did. She would never do to it what she had done to me.

She would never leave it.

"So...that's it, then. You've made up your mind, and there's nothing I can do or say it change it." I was narrating more to myself than to her, still in disbelief at the events that had just unfolded. "I guess I better go."

I planted my feet on the carpet and began to pull my jeans over my legs, past my thighs which had become prickly with goosebumps from the deathly chill that suddenly permeated the room. As I pulled the first sock over my left foot, she turned and grabbed the back of my shirt, hoisting herself unsteadily towards me. Desperation in her eyes, she planted her face into my chest and wept more plump tears.

"No…not yet…" she whispered in between tearful convulsions. "Let's just stay like this for a while…"

I put an arm around her, but could not bring myself to feel sympathy. I knew what she was going through, and I felt as she felt, but we were no more than strangers now, and this sort of vulnerability between us was no longer acceptable. If I thought of her as more than that, I knew it would be that much more difficult to deal with it. After a few more moments of silence, I knew I had to do what needed to be done. The time for despair, bargaining, and anger had passed and there was one option left for me.

"Anna…this is only going to make it worse. Let's just do it quickly and get it over with. You know, like a band-aid."

I gently but firmly grabbed her wrists and removed them from my neck and chest where they had come to rest and placed them back around the pillow which had become my substitute. Standing up, I felt along the floor for my shirt and began to button it up, slowly, savoring every second I could keep myself there.

Shoes, jacket, keys, wallet, cigarettes, phone; I ran through my checklist twice, to be sure, because I knew if I realized later that I had left something there, I would never see it again. With equal parts trepidation and exhaustion I hosted my trusty grey messenger back over my shoulder and offered her one last glance. It was just as well her face was buried in that pillow, because I had no idea what I'd actually say if her gaze caught mine. 'Goodbye' was too hard, 'I still love you' was too cruel, and 'I'll wait for you to realize that you've made a mistake' was too self-serving. Better to say nothing and be thought a fool, than to speak and remove all doubt.

I tip-toed cautiously past the foot of the bed and out into the hallway, hoping she hadn't heard my departure. The part of me that still loved her wanted to let her hide from reality; she could keep her face buried in that pillow for as long as she wanted, pretending I was still there. I winced for a moment as I considered my motives, desperately wishing I had been given an equitable option.

Passing into the living room, I stopped just short of the front door as I caught site of something out of my periphery. Nick was sleeping on the couch.

What the hell is he doing here?

Nick was Anna's ex-boyfriend, the guy she had dated immediately before me. He was a quite but fun-loving stoner. Traipsing about in that dirty hoodie of his, he was always on the lookout for two things: weed and the nearest party.

They had 'kept in touch' since they broke up six months ago. I knew the whole was bullshit; guys don't do the 'let's still be friends' thing, but they do do the 'pretending they are your friend and sticking around until your new boyfriend fucks up and you need a shoulder to cry on' thing. I had always been suspicious of him and resentful of his 'relationship' with Anna, but I couldn't blame him really. It was a textbook move and had I been in his position, I probably would have done the same damn thing. He was always pleasant enough to me, anyway.

Oh, that's right. He had kindly given Anna a ride home from the party last night after I had driven back to the apartment. She insisted on spending the night there, despite the fact there were no available beds or couches or anything approaching sleep-worthy except for the floor, and I was in no mood to argue with her about it while she was in her altered state. I told her to call me when she woke up from her drunken coma and I would come pick her up, but apparently she'd rather be riding with Nick. Why was *here*, though? *Why didn't he leave?*

I stood over Nick and watched him sleep for a few moments, the rhythmic rise and fall of his chest mirroring the beat of the shrill sobs coming from the bedroom, and found myself boiling with rage. What kind of sick bitch brings her ex-boyfriend over when she breaks up with you? No doubt as soon as I left, she'd run crying into his arms, and he'd be there to comfort her, poisoning her thoughts with 'oh, you're better off without him' and 'you're too good for him, he doesn't understand you like I do' sorts of garbage. *God, what a fucking asshole.*

Then I did something that I had wanted to do for years, but always feared the resulting consequences would be too great if I ever found the courage to. Now, I had nothing to lose.

I pulled my right arm back and sent my clenched fist flying into Nick's bristly jaw. The sick crack of bone against bone echoing loudly off the walls was followed by shouts of surprised pain as Nick's neck snapped to the side.

"What the fuck…?" he moaned, cradling his bloody lip with one hand and holding the other out defensively. He looked up at me through squinted eyes with a look of fear and horror.

"She's all yours," I spat, shaking the tension out of my hand, "Good fucking luck. You'll need it; round two with her ain't any easier."

I pushed my way out the front door before he could respond or retaliate and stepped out into the parking lot behind Anna's apartment building. The early morning sun shining down upon me cast a pale light over the scene, warming my bones as well as my spirit.

Yeah, everything's going to be alright.

Pulling my car door open with a careless yank, I tossed my bag into the passenger seat and hurriedly jammed the keys into the ignition. I revved the engine a few times as one final 'fuck you' to her neighbors, who had always annoyed me, and pulled out of the parking lot onto the side street running along the complex. I cranked the radio to full volume while pawing through my pockets for a cigarette, which proved difficult as my hands were still shaking from the adrenaline.

A few blocks down the boulevard, the indignant, self-righteous fury in my heart began to subside, and the anxious fear slowly started clawing it's way in. Rapidly scanning through the radio for an anthem to keep me focused, I happened to stumble upon a station that was playing 'our song', and then, in that car, I finally did what I hadn't allowed myself to do while I was still inside, with her.

I wept. Openly, and with abandon, tears streamed down my face. I didn't devolve into a blubbering, sniffling mess, but only because I was so far past that point that it didn't seem appropriate. I wasn't wallowing in self-pity, I hated myself. I hated that I was responsible for this. She was the only thing that ever mattered to me, and I had driven her away with my selfishness, just like before. Five long years had passed, but in the end, nothing had changed.

Eventually, my paranoia about being seen crying by other drivers while operating a motor vehicle got the best of me, and I pulled off to the side of the highway I wiped my eyes on my sleeves of my jacket and took a deep breath.

Okay. Where did my life go so horribly wrong?

CHAPTER 2

I met Anna when I was fifteen years old, during my sophomore year of high school. She and I had a few of our core classes together freshman year and I had always admired her from afar, but never worked up the courage to say anything to her or do anything about it. I accepted that I had missed my chance; fortune favored the bold, as they say.

My sophomore year I befriended a girl named Katie, who unbeknownst to me at the time, was Anna's best friend. Katie and I became close because we rode the same bus to and from school every day and had noticed each other in one of our classes together. Katie always seemed nice enough to me; she was one of those bubbly, blonde cheerleader-in-waiting types where you couldn't quite tell if their enthusiasm towards you was authentic, but I hadn't yet been rejected by enough women to have a good understanding of my 'place' or 'league, so I had a notion to pursue her. One afternoon in Chemistry class, I had decided to make a romantic overture towards her, but just before I could execute my awkward facsimile of what I believed to be appropriate courtship behavior, she turned to me and asked me a question that would change the rest of my life.

"Hey," she lowered her voice as she leaned closer to me, "do you remember a girl named Anna?"

"O-of course I do," I stumbled, taken completely by surprise by the mention of a girl of whom I hadn't thought of in nearly a year. "We had a few classes together last year."

"Well, I'm going to hang out with her after school." She fluttered her eyes and gave me a look that I couldn't resist, "You should come with."

My eyes widened and a bead of sweat trickled down my temple. I was in heaven. I didn't particularly have a preference between them yet; both Katie and Anna seemed like nice, cute girls whose innocence was ripe for the taking, and with the two of them conspiring together I liked my odds So of course, I agreed to go with her and in no short order, I found myself admiring Anna once more, just like old times. Only, this time, it wasn't from so far away. It was up close and personal.

We lived in different cities now, Anna and I. She had moved away after freshman year to go live with her father in a neighboring city, and only spent alternating weekends with her mother in the town where I lived. I was young and naive, and the ramifications of having a long-distance relationship — Anna only lived about 15 miles away, but when you don't have a car that still seems to be 'long distance'

— hadn't really occurred to me to be as problematic as they would ultimately prove to. I managed to convince myself that it might have even been for the best, really. I had a tendency to get bored easily in relationships, and this may have been a blessing in disguise: a way to keep things fresh and interesting between us. When you only see your partner a few times a month, you hardly find time to bicker about insignificant things or brood about how poorly they treat you. Our arrangement almost certainly prolonged the interaction between us, perhaps to our detriment.

I freely admit now that my favorite part of a relationship is 'the hunt'; the period of longing and uncertainty before the relationship is actualized where the aggressing party plots and schemes ways to seduce the object of their heart's desire. I was devious when it came to the hunt; when there was a girl I fancied I spent every waking moment thinking of ways to have my life intersect with hers in a covert fashion.

"Oh, fancy meeting you here!" I'd say. "How odd to run into a classmate outside of school. It must be fate."

I loved it. Maybe it's something about being goal-oriented, but I've always believed nothing easy was ever worth doing, and so the longer the hunt went on, the happier I was. As the great Groucho Marx said,

I would never join a club that would have someone like me for a member.

The hunt in our relationship lasted for about 2 weeks. We went on one date and were instantly enamored with each other. I didn't even have to open the first page in my book of dirty tricks, she just...liked me. I didn't understand it at the time, and I still don't, but I was almost...disappointed. If the story I had told myself about the necessity of effort in relationships was true, how could this be anything approaching meaningful?

We started going, officially, Christmas Eve of that year, and at first things were great. Anna was the first 'real' girlfriend I had, where the relationship consisted of more than simply eating together at lunch and holding hands in-between classes. We lost our virginity to each other, and shared a special connection that I had lived my entire life not knowing I did not have. It was comforting, for a time, but then I began to fear to losing it.

It was cold morning in January, when my life as I knew it began change. I was running a little late for school that day because my alarm hadn't gone off some reason. I was standing at the bus stop by my house, looking down the boulevard hoping to see the tell-tale cloud of smog in the distance that would signal the arrival of my chauffeur.

My hands, placed snuggly in the pockets of my hoodie to protect them against the biting morning cold, began to pulse with vibrations from my phone. A text message...from Katie?

">Are you at school yet?" She must have noticed I wasn't on the bus that morning.

">No, I'm getting on the bus now," I replied, while unconsciously handing my ticket to the bus driver and finding a free seat.

">I'll be by your locker when you get here. We need to talk."

Ulp. I swallowed hard and considered how to respond.

">Why? What's up?"

A beat of silence, and then...

">Just let me know when you get here."

This was strange behavior, even for her. What on earth could she want to talk to me about? Perhaps some subtle inflection was lost in the textual translation, but I had never heard her be so serious about anything for as long as I had known her. Was I about to have the quintessential teenage experience; being broken-up through proxy?

The bus ride seemed longer than usual, and every red light and that barred the bus's path further exacerbated my paranoia. Cold sweat dripped down my cheeks and neck. There was no way I could avoid this. It wasn't like if I just refused to talk to her it wouldn't be happening.

At long last, the school building came into view and I shuffled out the side door of the bus onto the sidewalk and began to slowly approach the side entrance of the school. My locker was on the other side of the building, in the north wing, so I would have a good walk to consider where I had went wrong.

Every group of students I passed by while I wandered down the main hall seemed to hush as I drew near, like they all somehow could sense the impending doom in my demeanor, or instinctively knew: *there's a guy on his death march.*

Finally, it all became too much to bear, and I staggered across the hall, slamming into the door to the men's room. I hurriedly entered an unoccupied stall and promptly threw up my morning breakfast. It wasn't a violent, spastic outburst, my body just seemed to be…shutting down. After the last bit of waste had left me, I washed my mouth out in the sink and steeled myself for what was to come.

CHAPTER 3

"...and then she said it was over. That she loved me, but it wasn't enough to make it work." I closed my eyes took a deep swig of my beer, the recounting of the morning's drama having left me rather parched.

"Jesus." Tyler muttered, "Sounds like a hell of a night."

He gave me a sincere but stoic look, a man's way of expressing sympathy without overexposing himself.

"Was this before or after she threw up all over herself?"

His comment brought a grim smile to my lips. "After. Way after."

I pressed my knuckles against the cold bottle on the table, phantom pains penetrating my fist as I recalled what came next.

"On my way out, I clocked Nick in the face while he was sleeping."

Tyler belly laughed. "Epic. Did it make you feel any better?"

"For about five minutes, yeah." I smiled sadly, staring my beer down.

"Hey, come on, man. Cheer up. You're better off without her. You were miserable with her too, and you know it."

"Yeah. You're right." I looked him in the eye as I took another drink. "How do I get her *back*?"

Tyler smiled again. "Alright, fine, ignore your best friend's relationship advice; god knows I can't make one work for longer than a month. But if there's one thing I DO know, it's how to make women want you."

Tyler was a master at picking up women. He had read all the books and listened to all the tapes about 'how to seduce women' until he had memorized everything there was to know about the opposite sex. He called himself a 'pick-up artist'. You might laugh at that label, but he took it all very seriously. He somehow deduced that love, romance, and courtship were all just elaborate board games, and if you knew how to 'stack the deck' as he put it, there was nothing you couldn't get away with. To him, talking to women was a sport. A sport he was very, very good at.

You wouldn't guess that by looking at him, either. He's was a short, painfully white, gangster wannabe, but he had a good head on his shoulders, and in the game of love, knowing is half the battle.

He spent most nights at bars and clubs, trolling for women. It might sound despicable, but he stopped doing it just for the sex a long time ago. Now it was just about the thrill, the adrenaline rush of the 'will-she-won't-she' back and forth that got him off. When a woman wasn't receptive to his advances, he just cut his losses and moved on to the next target. The rejection didn't even faze him anymore. He never lied – well, never about anything important, anyway – he never deliberately hurt anybody, he just loved making people want him. Beneath the hyper-competitive alpha-male exterior there was a really decent, kind-hearted guy, but he had convinced himself that those sorts of sentiments just got in the way of his game.

I understood. He was amongst a fellow hunter. Though I was nowhere near as skilled as he was with women, I could see the appeal of his lifestyle.

"So, what do I do, master?" I bowed my head slightly and raised my hands in supplication.

"Step one. Get over her. And as we both know, the best way to get over someone is get under someone else."

"So to get the girl, I have to not want her anymore?" I asked, ignoring his crass suggestion for a moment, in favor of exposing the contradiction that I knew already to be true.

Tyler arched his eyebrows, grinning like an idiot. "Isn't love magical?"

Tyler ordered us another round of drinks, skillfully chatting up our attractive waitress in the process. After coaxing me into doing a few shots of tequila, he moved around to my side of the table and threw an arm around my neck.

"Listen Dave, I know you don't approve of the way I do business, but you can't deny I get results."

"It's not that I don't approve, I just don't *think*—"

"I know, I know," Tyler interrupted, "You don't think you can do it. Or you think you *could*, you just don't *want* to. Yeah, whatever, I've heard all the excuses before, man, and from people a lot more capable than you, I might add. But you wanna know a secret?"

Tyler pulled my head down and leaned into my ear, his tone changed to a hushed whisper. Somehow, the whole bar seemed to quiet itself, in anticipation of the magician pulling back the curtain on his own illusion.

"*Anyone* can do what I do. It's *easy*." He pulled away and the background noise of the other people around faded back in. Tyler took another shot and drummed his finger tips against the table top. "Okay, buddy, here's what I'm gonna do for you. Men have killed to get the opportunity I am about to bestow upon you, okay? I am gonna be your *wingman* tonight."

I chuckled as he continued. "Do you understand what that means? I am giving you first pick of the women in here tonight." He gestured around the entire bar, as if he was a king surveying his kingdom.

"Look, over there. The HB 8 at the end of the bar, by the bathroom."

'HB' is pick-up artist shorthand for 'hot babe'. The number on the end indicates the objective level of physical attractiveness of the woman in question, on a scale of one to ten. The joke is, there *is* no HB 10.

"She's cute, right? Go talk to her."

I eyed the woman, sitting by herself at the end of the bar, sipping her bright green drink out of a martini glass. I felt disgusted.

"I...I can't. It's too soon. I can't even look at another woman right now."

"No? What's the harm in looking?"

"I just—"

"You don't think she's looking at other guys? I got ten bucks that says Anna took a real good 'look' at Nick right after you left."

My nostrils flared and my eyes narrowed as I looked at him, mouth slightly agape. His words pierced me and brought my blood to a boil, but I swallowed hard and turned back towards the woman. I couldn't hate him for what he said, because I knew, in my heart of hearts, that he was right.

"There you go. See? It's not so bad. Man, she's smoking. Looks lonely too. Maybe her date stood her up."

We turned back to our drinks and began to develop our plan.

"Okay. Here's the deal. You're gonna go and talk to her for ten minutes, and then I'm gonna come over and try pull you away. Just roll with it, okay?"

"But what do I say?"

"It doesn't matter what you say to her. All that matters is how you say it. Don't act confident, BE confident. You're a good looking guy, David," he said, brushing off some dirt my shoulder. "You have every right to act like you're hot shit." His gaze became intense, like he was trying to imprint his knowledge onto my soul. "Just. Be. Yourself."

"I...but..."

Before I could concoct any cowardly excuse to free myself from his scheme, he stood up, ruffled my hair, and began walking away.

"Get out of your head. You're gonna be great. I believe in you."

Tyler slid up to a young blonde woman at the other end of the bar, and began chatting her up. Almost immediately, she began laughing and giggling and playfully pushing against his shoulder. It was absurd how good he was at this.

I took a deep breath and stood up from the table. Shutting out my nagging insecurities, I let my mind go quiet as I slowly approached the woman Tyler had picked out for me. The noise of the bar and its patrons melted away and I saw only her. I envisioned myself talking to her, and, in this fantasy world, she was putty in my hands.

PUAs — pick-up artists — refer to this as being 'in state'. Projecting your identity from a natural state of confidence and authenticity was the key to ensnaring women. It was hard to be friends with Tyler for so long without learning a few things about the trade.

"Hi. Mind if I join you?" I pulled up a bar stool and sat next to the woman without waiting for a response. It didn't really matter if she said yes or no, we were talking and that's all that mattered.

"No, I suppose not." The woman smiled slyly and fluttered her eyelashes. She really was gorgeous. The tight black dress she was wearing accentuated her petite build and long legs. She had long brown hair and her eyes were dark, almost black even. There was something very mysterious about her.

"So," I began. She sipped the last drop of her green drink and I motioned to the bartender to bring us another round. "What's a nice looking girl like you doing in a seedy dive like this?"

"Oh," she replied listlessly, a smile forming at the corner of her lips, "the same thing you're doing here, I imagine."

Not likely.

She suddenly burst into laughter. "I'm sorry. Does that line ever really work? What does it look like I'm doing?"

I smiled widely. "You're right. It was pretty terrible, wasn't it?" Slowly, I took a sip of my beer, regaining my momentum. "You look like you're waiting for someone. Boyfriend stand you up?"

"No, not really, just unwinding after a long day at work." She sipped her drink again.

"What do you do?" Women like it when you ask questions, but PUAs make it a rule to only ask questions you are legitimately curious about. This makes it easier to appear interested and authentic.

"I'm a paralegal at a law firm downtown."

"That must be tough. I've always heard lawyers dress up in nice suits and yell a lot and get to take home the big bucks while the paralegals do all the hard work."

She smiled and ran her hand through her hair. Perfect. People in secretarial positions always have insecurities about their careers.

"You've heard right. They get to play in court all day and then go home while we get stuck with the paper work. It's annoying, but it pays the bills, I guess."

"And that's what it's all about right?" I ventured, a hint of sarcasm draping my words. Enough to let her think I thought I could give her something more, but not so much as to make her think I wasn't being sincere.

"It's a damn big part of 'it'." She said confidently. "And what do you do, then? I suppose you haven't 'sold out'."

I reclined in my seat and smirked. "I'm a writer."

"Oh? And what do you write about?" she leaned backwards, her body language mirroring mine.

"Well, miss..." I stumbled for a second, but quickly recovered. "I'm sorry, I didn't catch your name. I'm David, by the way." I held out a hand and she took it in hers, squeezing it firmly as she smiled.

My eyes grew wide for a moment as she responded, "I'm *Anna*."

"Of course you are." Suddenly, I felt a third presence glide up behind me at the bar.

"Hey! David!" It was Tyler. Ten minutes, just like he said. "Dude, you've GOTTA come meet this chick. Her name's Jennifer, and she is a *legit* swimsuit model. She's invited us to a party on a house boat down at the pier. She is good to GO, my man."

His eyes were wide with excitement, but I knew it was all a ploy. I had caught a glimpse of her at the bar, and there was no way in hell she was a model.

I didn't even turn my head to look at her and replied, "I'm good, man. I'm having a nice talk with this young lady. Tyler, this is Anna."

"Anna. Wow." I nodded at him and we shared the delicious irony for a moment. "I'll, uh, I'll leave you two alone. It...it was great to meet you."

She raised her glass. "And you. Join us, won't you? And bring your blonde bimbo friend. I'd simply love to meet her." It was astonishing to see a woman actually capable of throwing Tyler off his rhythm. He sensed he was losing it and quickly snapped back.

"Thanks, but we're actually just about to head out. David, you gonna be okay to get home on your own?"

I turned back to Anna and looked into her eyes. "I'll get a cab."

Tyler nodded and turned back towards the bar. He gave me a quick, knowing wink as if to say 'you're the man', and rejoined the blonde girl. She wrapped herself around his arm and they stepped out the door, giggling and laughing, into the night. I knew they were never going to make it to that party...if it even existed.

"I'm sorry about him," I started, "he's...a bit of a Casanova. Nice guy, though, really."

"Mmhmm. And you're nothing like him, right?" she mused, lighting a cigarette.

"Well..." I grinned, bashfully. "I'm a *little* like him."

CHAPTER 4

Every step grew heavier as I entered the north wing of my school. With every inch of ground I gained, my backpack grew a hundred pounds heavier, and it felt like my legs were bound together with cast iron chains. I rounded the last bend, and looked to my locker. There was a throng of people crowded around, as though they were spectators waiting to watch a tight-rope walker fall to their death. I pushed my way through the crowd, and then I saw her. Katie. She was sitting on the ground, her back against my locker.

She was...crying?

Suddenly, I felt an intense sense of shame and guilt. Maybe everything in the world wasn't about me and the horrible dramas I played out in my head. Maybe, sometimes, talking was just something normal people did when they had a problem. Maybe rather than fearing these types of interactions, I would be a little happier, a little more functional as a human being, if I chose to embrace them instead.

I threw my backpack off and knelt down by her side, putting a hand on her shoulder.

"Katie...!" I shouted, uncertainty shaking my voice, "What's wrong...?"

She looked up at me, clutching the crumbled up tissue in her right hand tightly for just a moment before casting it a side and throwing her arms around me.

"Oh god, David, I am so sorry..."

"Hey," I said calmly, "It's going to be okay, alright?" I fished a tear out of the corner of her eye, and helped her to her feet. She smiled half-heartedly, rubbing her nose on the sleeve of her jacket.

"Thank you..." "Don't mention it," I replied, "Now, why don't you tell me what's wrong?"

"It's Anna..." she cried, the tearful sobs returning with gusto.

Oh no.

"What...?"

No. No no no no. Please, god, don't do this to me. Anything but this.

"She's...she's in the hospital."

The crowd around us began to dissipate as Katie wrapped her arms around me, sensing their bloodlust would not be sated today. I let my arms fall against her back and held her tightly as she sobbed gently into my jacket.

"No... No, It can't be... What happened...? Is she going to be okay...?"

"Last night," Katie began, pulling herself away from me, "we were hanging out with some guy friends of mine..."

No.

She looked to floor as she continued her story, oblivious to the fire in my eyes, the fury spreading through my face. "...and we started to smoke in the back my Mom's van..."

NO.

"Suddenly, she started freaking out...like she was having a seizure or something. Greg and Andrew ran away, but I was sober enough to call an ambulance... The doctors said they found traces of cocaine, ecstasy, meth, and barbiturates in her system... We don't know how they got there, we think the pot might have been laced... She was unconscious for a while, but it looks like she's gonna pull through..."

She swallowed hard and looked up at me, searching for signs of a response. I did not give the one she wanted.

"You...stupid fucking bitch."

"W-what?" She recoiled, clearly shocked by my rancor.

"I can't fucking believe you. And you're supposed to be her friend? How could you fucking do this to her?!" Looking back now, I will admit directing my anger towards her probably wasn't the most productive or logical course of action, but someone...someone had to take responsibility for this. This had to be someone's fault.

"H-hey, fuck you asshole!" She retorted, "Why are you getting mad at me?!"

"They were your drugs, weren't they?! You put her in danger!"

"I didn't make her do anything she didn't want to! I saved her life!"

I glared at her through narrow eyes, but didn't speak another word. I considered her plight for the briefest of moments before deciding blame could be laid later; now was a time for action.

"Where is she?"

"I told you, the hospital..."

"*What* hospital?!"

"I don't know, they wouldn't let me ride in the ambulance with her! A growl welled up in the back of my throat; I was on the verge of going berserk.

"Goddammit, Katie!"

I pulled open my locker and shoved my backpack inside and then slammed it back shut before running off.

"Where are you going?!" Katie called after me.

"I'm going to find my fucking girlfriend."

I burst out of the main entryway and ran along the sidewalk, considering heading back down to take the bus, but knew that running on adrenaline I could get to Anna's house well before the bus would even make start making its round.

As I marched up the hill towards Anna's house, a torrent of emotions spiraled around in my brain. What should I be feeling? Pity? Fear? Anger, even? I freely admit now what I was too scared to come to terms with then; that I was angry at what had happened, angry at her for doing this to herself, and angry at myself for not having seen it coming.

I knew Anna did drugs. How couldn't she? She was an 'average' teenager in virtually every sense of the word, how could she not at least flirt with the debauchery and sin that was practically a staple of 'growing up'?

I didn't, of course, take part in any of those kinds of rites of passage. I told myself I was above polluting myself with toxic substances just to escape my own existence, but really, I was just scared. Scared that this would happen.

Wrestling with my thoughts made the time fly by, and before I knew it I was standing in front of Anna's house. I raced up to the front door and began to bang away, hoping that somebody, anybody would be inside to give me some answers.

A few seconds passed, and I banged again, harder this time, trying to break the door down. Still no response. I checked the drive way and found it to be empty. Of course they're not home. They're at the hospital. With their nearly dead daughter.

Where I should be.

A sudden sense of desperation and futility washed over me, and I began to feel tired. I fell to my knees, hyperventilating and exhausted, and found I could stand to be conscious no longer. Curling up on the welcome mat of Anna's house, I closed my eyes, and let myself sleep.

I awoke some hours later to my cell phone ringing. Frantically, I dug it out my pocket and held it to my ear.

"Hello?!" I practically shouted, desperately hoping that someone who knew something that would help me figure out what to do would be on the other line.

"David? It's Sally." Aunt Sally and Uncle Trip were my caretakers at the time. My parents had died when I was young and Trip, my father's brother, had graciously agreed to take me in for a while.

"Oh..." I replied, sounding more disappointed than I meant to.

"Where are you? It's almost five..."

I looked to the sky, which had begun to darken as the sun grew smaller behind the horizon. The road by Anna's house had grown busy with the sounds of afternoon traffic. How long had I been out?

"I'm...at Anna's place." It wasn't a lie, exactly.

"Oh...are you staying there for dinner?"

"No," I mumbled as I hoisted myself off the welcome mat, rubbing the checkered imprint off my cheek. "I'm coming home now."

It was around 8:30 when Anna finally called me that night.

"Hi..." she said, shyly.

"Hi." I replied, coldly. I still hadn't decided how I was going to play this one, but I was so angry, at her, at the world, at myself, that I just couldn't contain it.

"So, I guess you heard..." she continued.

"Yeah, thank god Katie had the decency to fill me in, or else I might never have known my girlfriend almost died last night!"

"You're mad." Clearly, she was confused by my reaction. I decided to go with it.

"You're fucking right I'm mad. How could you do this to me, Anna? How the fuck could you?!"

"To you?!" She cried back, "You're not the one who spent the night in a hospital!"

"You think I wasn't in there with you?! You think I wasn't every bit as scared as you were?! You don't exist in a vacuum, Anna! Things you do to yourself affect the people that love you, too!"

"Yeah, it sure sounds like you *love* me a whole lot, David! I go through a near-death experience and you're arguing with me over which one of us was more affected by it! You haven't even asked me if I'm okay..."

I swallowed and took a deep breath. She was right. There was a time for principles and morality, but this was not it.

"I'm sorry, I just... I was so scared; I didn't know what to do. I thought I had lost you... This was really hard for me, I hate feeling powerless."

"Oh, I'm sorry, it was hard for you, was it?! Well, I'm so sorry that me nearly dying today was so hard on you!"

We didn't really reach any sort of amicable conclusion to our conversation last night. We yelled and cried and said we loved each other but nothing seemed to fix anything. Something had changed in our relationship that night; something had begun to eat away at it from within.

We tried to pretend everything was okay for a while, but once it became clear that Anna was 'okay' physically, mentality, and so on her parents deigned it appropriate to ground her. As if her near-death experience hadn't been a lesson learned deeply enough.

No leaving the house unsupervised, no visitors, no phone calls was their rule. I was completely cut off from her; except for e-mail and the occasional phone call late at night after her parents had gone to bed. In truth, it probably saved our relationship for a time; it gave it a 'forbidden' exoticness that probably kept us from drifting apart immediately. I was one of her only ties left to the outside world, and I, for all my brow-beating and posturing and self-righteous indignation, still loved her.

After a few months, the novelty of the 'long-distance relationship' began to wane, and we both became interested in other people. I had started to see another girl in my Chemistry class, Maria, who was, because of her zealously religious upbringing, decidedly anti-drug, and she became interested in Nick, a friend who lived across the street from her, and was able to sneak visits with her far more conveniently than I was.

It was the last day of school before summer break when she told me that it was over. I was at my house, after school, playing video games with my friend Chris. We were in the middle of shooting zombies when my phone rang. I sighed deeply as I checked to see who it was from. I probably should have known things were approaching conflict, when just the idea of talking to my girlfriend on the phone filled with me dread and anxiety. I passed the controller to Chris and took my phone into the next room before I answered it.

"Hey baby, what's up?" I said, rather hurriedly. I was desperate to get back to the zombie holocaust. We had just gotten to the last level, and if Chris beat the King Zombie while I was out of the room I was going to throw a temper tantrum.

"David...we need to talk." She sounded collected, not too serious or upset, so I assumed the topic at hand would be something clerical.

"Okay. What are we going to talk about?"

"I...I don't think it's working out between us." Her voice quivered ever so slightly at the first word, but quickly regained composure.

"What?" I replied, blankly.

"Things haven't been good between us for a while now, David. You know that."

"I do?" I replied again.

I didn't necessarily disagree, but I wasn't aware we had placed this realization into collective knowledge. Things hadn't been good for me, sure, but I had made peace with that. I could live with things that 'aren't good' as long as I had hope that they would 'get better'. I guess I just didn't realize things weren't good for her too.

"We barely talk anymore, we never see each other, whenever I try to talk to you, you just...pull away."

She was right. I had abandoned the relationship months ago when I met Maria. I hadn't been unfaithful to Anna, in the technical term of the phrase, but in practicality, Anna was no longer my girlfriend.

"You're right, Anna. You're right." I said, realizing I was on the verge of losing what I had taken for granted for all those months. How I was I to know she wouldn't always be there? It had never occurred to me that I might lose the thing I thought I needed most. "I've been selfish and distant and cold and I am so sorry for putting you through all of this. This situation we've been in these past few months has been hard for me – I know it's been hard for you too – but I just haven't figured out how to deal with it. *I love you, Anna.*"

Quiet sobs trickled through the receiver. "God, I was so prepared to be such a bitch about all this, but I just can't... I love you, David, I'm sorry..."

She had made up her mind, and there was no convincing her otherwise. That was one thing I loved about Anna. When she made up her mind about something, there was absolutely nothing you could do to change it. No amount of empirical evidence, witty turn of phrase, or downright begging would cause her to compromise, even in the face of oblivion. There was no way she could want to leave me, even if things weren't great at the moment, but she knew that it was time, that it was what was best for everyone involved, and bizarrely, I respected that.

"Can we still be friends...?" She managed through her sobs.

"I... I don't think so, Anna." I responded calmly. I was in an emotional coma, shocked by the events folding around me, so my higher, rational brain had taken control. "I don't think that would work. I love you too much to be able to hide my feelings. I couldn't live that *lie*."

Her sobs intensified and I listened to her cry for a few minutes, completely unsure of what to do or say. I had bought into her premise. It was over, and there was no going back, and I was going to burn every bridge I could on my way out.

"I...I have to go..." she whispered again.

I knew she didn't have to go, but I didn't confront her about it. There was nothing to be gained from it, this exchange was over, and all that was left was for us to realize it and hang up the phone. So I did.

"Goodbye, Anna."

I put the phone back into my pocket and went back into the room where Chris was. I sat back down next to him on the couch and he offered the game controller back to me. I wasn't sure if he had heard the conversation or not, but there was an undertone of consolation in his gesture. I accepted it in the spirit in which it was given and focused on the television screen. If I couldn't have love, I could have anger and hate and glory on this virtual battlefield, and maybe in a way, that would be sufficient.

I was gonna kill the fuck out of these zombies.

CHAPTER 5

Tick. Tock. Tick. Tock. Tick.

It seems to get louder each time. Each successive rotation of the second hand more pronounced than the one preceding it until it becomes a deafening echo. Every tick you hope that maybe -- just maybe -- you won't be conscious to hear the tock...but you will. The tock is the taunt; the punchline to the joke at your expense. It will drive you mad, if you let it.

You've memorized every crack, every imperfection, every nook and cranny in the ceiling. You've counted each little paint bubble over a thousand times by now. No amount of inane repetitive tasks can force you into the peaceful slumber you long for.

Then, the sleep-deprived hallucinations will begin.

Shapes and colors begin to materialize against the white paint. Your cartoon bears and stuffed dinosaurs begin to crackle to life, locking arms and joyously singing old bible songs. The television screen warps and contorts and snaps, causing the deadpan uncharismatic news anchor within to spill forth onto your carpet.

You look over at your partner. They sleep so soundly. You can barely even hear them breathing...how nice it must be for them. They take for granted things as simple and natural for them as sleep. What would they do if they suddenly found themselves unable to escape into that peaceful oblivion they rely on for so much?

When you have insomnia, you never have that peaceful period of rest and regeneration bookending each period of accomplishment; you just fade in and out between states of complacent paralysis and groggy somnambulation.

It was late when the dull pounding sensation in my temple finally outweighed the fear of the nauseous turning in my stomach. How much had I drank last night? I rolled out of bed and slowly put my feet on the cold floor. Gradually, things began to come into focus. I was in my apartment. Clothes were strewn everywhere and a haunting whistle echoed off the high ceiling; it was coming from the bathroom, steam billowing from the crack underneath the door.

Oh, right. Anna. I hadn't even noticed her get up in my comatose tranquility.

A small surge of adrenaline urged me to jump in the shower with her and pick up where we left off last night, but the room was spinning far too much for me to even contemplate capitulating to my hormones.

I noticed her purse sitting on an armchair in the living room and decided I needed a cigarette to calm my nerves. I began rummaging through her possessions and suddenly came across her wallet. I eyed it suspiciously for a few moments before deciding to open it. Somehow, I had forgotten to ask her age at any point during the night's proceedings – a rookie mistake. She seemed young, not too young, but with all the human growth hormone in the milk these days you never can be too sure.

I thumbed through the various plastic cards – credit cards, library card, supermarket membership – until at last I found it: her driver's license. I frantically scanned it for her date of birth and hoped my drunken stupor wouldn't impair my basic mathematic skills. 2009 minus 1986... whew, she's legal, thank god. Releasing my bated breath, I moved to place the ID back into her wallet, when suddenly, something stopped me. I looked at the ID again.

This was an ID for someone named Sarah Lewis. *Who the hell is Sarah Lewis?* A fake ID, maybe? No...there was something else going on here, and I was going to get to the bottom of it.

I walked back towards the bathroom. She was out of the shower, standing naked in front of the sink, drying her hair.

"Hey, Sarah?"

"Hey, handsome." She turned, smiling wryly for a moment. Then her eyes went wide with fear as she realized the jig was up.

"...Who are you?"

The sexy listlessness in her voice evaporated as she moved into the bedroom and began dressing herself. "Ask your buddy, Tyler," she said, coldly.

"What does Tyler have to do with—" I thought aloud, but almost immediately I knew what had happened. "Get out."

Anna – no, Sarah, now – flung her high heels over her shoulder and collected her purse before stepping out the front door of my apartment, slamming the door shut behind her. I took a second, to try and calm myself, but as soon as I heard the door close I leapt across the bed and dug around in my jeans from last night. I fished my cell phone out of my back pocket and hit speed dial two.

"Yo! My man, how'd it go last night? You sealed the deal, didn't you? I'm so proud...my little protégé."

"You are un-fucking-believable." I said, incredulously. "You hired a hooker to sleep with me because you thought it would help me get over my break up." I wasn't mad, so much as in awe of his dastardly plot.

"Fuck! How'd you find out? I paid her good money to make sure she kept her mouth shut!"

"I went through her purse, looking for her smokes. Found her ID. Sarah, was it?"

He chuckled before responding, "Damn! Oh well. I thought that the whole 'Anna' thing might be a little much, but fuck man, when I dream, I dream big."

"You are diabolical." I wanted to hate him for deceiving me, but I knew his intentions were good. Despite finding out the whole thing was a farce, I couldn't deny how talking to the woman at the bar last night made me feel. It was the rush, the hunt that I had missed for so long. I needed it now more than ever. I needed more.

"I know. But hey, this is no time to feel sorry for yourself. She would have slept with you even if I hadn't paid her; I just took out some…insurance." There was a clinical aloofness to his voice that chilled me to my bone. "Think of it this way: step one is complete. We move on to phase two tonight. 9:30 at The Escapade. Be there."

I was about to respond when the sounds of pleasured moans started echoing through the receiver

"Look, I'm a little busy right now, man. I gotta go. See you tonight." Click.

I smiled quietly to myself. "That brilliant bastard."

Suddenly, the sick welled up in the back of my throat and I rushed to the bathroom to pray to the porcelain god. It was one of the bad ones. One of the pukes where you're not sure you're going to make it out alive, so you'd pray for the end if only you didn't fear being found dead from choking on your vomit. After my stomach emptied itself and the whirlpool of water had sucked it down the drain, I curled up on the floor mat and checked my watch. 9:30. Plenty of time to sleep it off before the night's festivities.

I awoke sometime around noon and took a shower, dressed myself, and went into town to get something to eat. After vomiting up yesterday's lunch and dinner I felt like I was starving. I passed an old diner that Anna and I used to eat at all the time — we loved cheesy joints like that — but decided the last thing I needed right then was to sit in the booth we used to sit in, eat the food we used to eat, and stare out into the street, people watching me like we used to. I still was trying to grasp the concept of sleeping in a bed that she no longer slept in with me.

"Your team," she'd say, pointing out any time a remarkably ugly or strange-looking person passed by on the side walk. It was this game we played. I was always horrible at it, and thought it a little cruel and childish, but the fact she didn't see me the way she saw all those *ordinary* people...it made me feel good. It made me feel like I was worth something. But now, I realized how fleeting all that was. A different time, a different place, and I might be walking past that same diner, and she might be placing me on Nick's team.

I stopped in at *Samswiches*, a sandwich shop owned by a middle-aged stoner turned entrepreneur named Sammy. It was a great place: they made the best turkey clubs in the whole city. Anna and I never went there as much as I would have liked because she got really terrible food poisoning one time she ordered the 'vegetarian sub'. I had heard once that the vegetarian sub was just a joke; that the cooks always did terrible things to the food when people ordered it as sort of a 'fuck you' to the trendy hipsters that ate that sort of garbage, but I never confided that in Anna. I guess I didn't want to believe that her predilection towards 'eating healthy' was as misguided as it may have eventually turned out to be. She certainly didn't *need* to eat healthy. She was skinny as a twig, yet she always fussed about her weight. I tried and tried again to reassure her, to let her know that she was beautiful and sexy just the way she was, but I guess we can't save people from themselves.

I ordered the meatball sub that day. I needed something warm in my stomach because the deathly chill that haunted Anna's apartment that fateful day seemed to have spread throughout the entire city. I couldn't remember a day this cold in September for as long as I had lived there. Maybe it was a sign. Or maybe it was just global warming.

I say on a bench in park that day and ate my lunch. The chill had little effect on the amount of pedestrian traffic through the park that day, just the speed at which people moved. Business men and women in suits hurried alongside students through the plaza to get on the street cars to take them through the city to their destinations.

Taking another bite of the sandwich, I practiced an old PUA exercise in eye contact that Tyler had taught me years ago. The idea is to practice making eye contact with every woman you see and hold it until they break it. The idea is to make eye contact with every woman you see, and hold it until they break it. The exercise is designed to build confidence. You don't have to do anything, just look at them until they look away first, and then you're done. Move onto the next one. I didn't really understand how or why, but just being able to look at women made them seem easier to approach. They were no different from us, really. They wanted the same things guys did, they just had different socially-acceptable ways of going about it.

Some women smiled at me, some shook their heads in disgust, and some just ignored me outright. The trick was to not let any of their reactions phase you. If they smiled, then great, but you didn't need them to because you're a high-value guy that's used to that king of attention from women, so it wasn't a big deal. Likewise, it they snubbed you, then so what? You have no shortage of options and they probably weren't worth your time anyway. It was the ones that didn't know what to think that always intrigued me the most. Were they really that thrown off by simple human kindness?

By the time I had finished my sandwich I had forgotten all about Anna. There were so many beautiful, intelligent, sexy women in this city. Why was I so hung up on this particular one? Tyler had told me one time that when it came to women it was always easier to start fresh with a new one than repair damage with an old one. Forget about trying to seduce, no, 'attract' — Pick-up Artists like Tyler were very particular about the terminology surrounding their 'skill set', even pick-up artist was a crass term, 'Venusian artist' was preferred — women you already have some sort of relationship with, romantic or otherwise. It was easier to start with a clean slate and make a masterpiece than to try and overwrite something that was already there. *The end is where I would begin.*

CHAPTER 6

When Anna dumped me in 10th grade, I wasn't sure I would ever recover. At first I tried to shrug it off and hide it from my friends, who teased me about my sensitivity to the whole thing. But in truth I was truly shocked by the sensation, not so much that it happened, but at how it made me feel. I finally understood the idea of 'heartbreak,' because quite literally, my chest hurt. There was a gaping Anna-shaped chasm in my soul and I didn't think I would ever be able to fill it again.

I grew depressed and my grades began to plummet. Trip and Sally thought it was just a rebellious phase I was going through and that if they yelled at me enough or sent me to enough child psychologists I would outgrow it, in time. But I never did. I never got over Anna. The anger and loneliness festered inside me over the summer and I became increasingly detached from the rest of the world. Life didn't seem worth living if I couldn't be with her.

I stopped going out with friends and stayed in on Saturday nights, reading books and watching movies and playing games, anything that could distract from the crippling emptiness long enough to get through the day. My relationships with my peers crumbled, and by the time junior year rolled around I found I was completely without friends.

Telling myself I needed to take whatever measures were necessary to get over her, I set out in search of someone else to fill the void in my heart. If I couldn't have Anna, I would get someone who was nothing like her just to show her how much I didn't need her. And that first day, in junior English class, my eyes fell upon my target.

Courtney leaned over to me. "Hey, my pen just ran out of ink. Can I borrow one from you?"

I had seen Courtney around school before. She was one of those 'free-spirit' hippie types. She was fiercely devoted to environmental preservation and was a talented thespian in our school's seasonal plays. She was nothing like the 'type' of girl I would usually go for, but there was something about the way she carried herself, that she was a whole person on her own and didn't care what anyone thought that captivated me. I was going to have to play this one just right, I thought. No admiring from afar this time around. I was going to have to take some bold action.

I reached into my bag and pulled out a pen and handed it to Courtney without saying a word.

"Thanks," she whispered. Not five seconds after handing it to her, the pen fell apart in her hand.

"Oh shit! I'm sorry!" she practically shouted. The teacher paused her lecture for a moment and gave us a stern look.

I chuckled before handing her a new pen. "It's okay. That was only my *favorite pen*. Don't worry about it." She swallowed hard and looked me over, uncertain if I was joking or not. The hunt was on.

"You'll have to make it up to me, somehow. Buy me lunch?"

And that was that. Courtney and I were dating by the end of the week. Everything had gone according to plan. Except...except, well...it quickly became apparent to me why I didn't go for girls like Courtney.

She was dumb as a post. Bless her heart, she was kind and sweet, but she just didn't have a lick of common sense. It got so bad that we got to the point where when we'd do our homework together she wouldn't let me look at her essays because she felt so intimidated by how good mine were by comparison. I also didn't find her particularly sexually attractive. She wasn't hideous to look at or anything, I just...I don't know. The spark just wasn't there.

Our relationship continued for a few months while we both pretended that things were okay, but we both know knew they really weren't. Eventually I accepted that my gambit had backfired and we agreed to split up, under mostly amicable terms, and we remained friends for a good long while, but every time I looked at her I knew why our relationship didn't go the distance. She wasn't Anna.

And really, that's what I had been looking for; an Anna placeholder, someone to keep the seat warm until she came back to me, and that's how I lived my life for the next five years. Never taking any chances, never seizing any opportunities, and never doing anything, because I thought I had to be ready. At any moment, she could walk through that door and be mine again. If that didn't happen because I'd moved to California to go to college, or traveled abroad in Europe, I'd never forgive myself. I just bided my time, and waited.

In the end, my waiting paid off. I saw Anna at a party, the year I turned 19. It was surprising, but it didn't sting nearly as much as I told myself it would. I was just so happy to see her, to know that she was safe and happy, and that the years hadn't drained her life force from her the way they had mine.

We chatted for a while, and remained in touch over the next few months. She worked the graveyard shift while going to school during the day, so she never had anyone awake to talk to. We'd text back and forth every now and then, and even meet up for coffee one in a while. I was happy with our arrangement, because it was safe. I got to see her, but she couldn't really hurt me; she was in a relationship now – with Nick – and I wasn't prepared to make any sort of advances that could compromise that.

After a few months of intermittent contact she showed up at my apartment one night, and we had coffee and talked like we had many times before, but this time something was amiss. We started talking about the past, about us, and about what had gone wrong so many years ago.

"Why do you think I've kept talking to you all these months...?" she asked sadly, wiping away tears forming at the corners of her eyes.

"I don't know...nostalgia?" I ventured, uncertain what she wanted me to say. Was I really too proud to admit I still loved her, even after all this time?

She shook her head in disgust, offended by my comment. "I still care about you, David... I still want you to be a part of my life."

I headed her off at the pass, making sure the lines were drawn. I still wasn't prepared to take second place in this contest. "It's too hard for me to be 'just friends'. I can't just forget how I feel about you..."

"So you still love me?" she asked, her eyes twinkling in the moonlight.

This is it. This is the fulcrum on which your entire existence has been balanced. Choose your next words carefully.

"Of course. I always have, and I always will, Anna."

She wrapped her arms around me. "I'm so afraid..." she cried, "I'm so afraid that I made a huge mistake when I was young and that I'll spend the rest of my life paying for it."

My heart broke. I knew exactly what she meant. I leaned in and pressed my lips against hers. They were warm, and sweet, and tasted just like I remembered them. She wrapped her arms around my neck and held me, but pushed me away when I started fumbling with her belt.

"No, I can't...! Nick..."

You are so close. Don't let some burnout fuck up stand between you and what you want. I was desperate, so I pulled out the most sinister trick in my bag. This was my last resort.

"Please..." I whispered, softly. "Just let me make you feel good...one last time."

I was startled and horrified by my words, but I would do or say anything to get her back. It sounds horrible now, I realize, but when you truly believe you are someone's soul mate, all evils are justified. *I did what I had to do.*

She breathed deeply and relaxed in my arms, and then we made love. It was neither pleasurable nor nostalgic for me; it was just like I was playing a game. This was something I had to do. This was part of my plan.

Anna fell asleep on the couch afterwards and I found I was so disgusted with both her and myself, that I left her in the living room and crawled under the covers of my bed, where I hid until morning. She woke me after the run rose with gentle kisses on my neck and climbed onto me for round two.

We lay in bed for a few hours holding each other before she had to leave to go to class. I kissed her goodbye, and prayed that that would be the last I saw of her. Now when I looked at her I would no longer see the beautiful innocent little girl I fell in love with, I would only see the cheating slut that I myself had turned her into. Each man kills the thing he loves, and I had killed my love with a kiss and a flattering word. She was gone forever.

I wrote her a letter, telling her that that night had been a mistake, and that we shouldn't see each other anymore. That it wasn't too late for her to patch things up with Nick. That she deserved more than I was able to give. I dropped the letter off at her apartment that afternoon and thought that it was finally all over.

I was wrong.

CHAPTER 7

It was almost 9:30, and I had been waiting in-line at the Escapade for about an hour. Fucking Tyler, I'm sure if he had just agreed to meet beforehand he could have gotten me into the club without even trying, but on my own, I'm just an average guy.

I breathed into my palms and rubbed them together. I was in a jacket and freezing my ass off; I had no idea how some of the women in the line, clad in miniskirts and halter tops weren't dying of frostbite.

My cell phone vibrated in my pocket and I dug it out, a text message from Tyler.

">Where R U?"

">In line. Be there soon." I typed back, the cold nipping at my finger tips.

">Lines 4 losers lol. just grab a chick and walk in like you own the place."

I sighed and closed my phone. He was right. I looked along the line for a suitable candidate. There were two women directly behind me, a blonde and a red-head, who looked like they were about to freeze to death.

"Hey," I turned and spoke to them, motioning to my arms, "Grab on and let's go in."

"Um...What?" The red-head turned to her friend, each giving the other skeptical looks.

"Trust me."

They reluctantly grabbed onto my arms and we stepped out of the line. Approaching the roided-up bouncer at the front of the line, I swallowed a lump in my throat and gave him a friendly nod. He looked us over for a few seconds suspiciously, and then smiled, lifting the rope gateway that barred our passage into the warm of the club.

We entered and I began searching for Tyler, which was no easy task through a veritable sea of people and flashing strobe lights.

"Wow, you did it!" The blonde on my right screamed over the blaring dance music.

"Thanks!" The redhead chimed in.

"Don't thank me," I called back, spotting the man I had been searching for. I let the women go and started to make a beeline through the crowd. "Thank Tyler."

Passing awkwardly between dancing couples and groups of trapped people, I made my way to the end of the bar, to the VIP sections where I saw Tyler sitting.

"Hey! There he is!" Tyler shouted, getting up from the booth and throwing his arms around me.

"It worked. Your stupid trick actually worked!" I yelled into his ear.

"Nah, it didn't," he laughed, "I told the bouncer to let in any awkward looking guys with leather jackets. But it felt good, right? Here, have a drink."

I rolled my eyes as Tyler handed me a shot of clear liquid. We each downed our drink in unison.

"Woo!" Tyler called out, grimacing. "That'll put some hair on your balls. Here, I got some people I want you to meet." He lead me back to the booth where he was sitting with a few other people.

"Ladies, if you'll excuse us, we've got some guy business to discuss."

Three women, each more stunningly gorgeous than the one before her, smiled and stood up from the table, winking shyly at Tyler before dispersing among the crowd.

"Exchange students," Tyler smirked, "Gotta love 'em. Come on, man, sit down."

I sat down next to Tyler, across from two other guys, who looked like they belonged in an Abercrombie and Fitch catalogue.

"Darren, Rick, this is David, my third pupil for this evening."

"Nice to meet you," I shouted across the table.

Darren and Rick each nodded, sizing me up. Clearly they were not happy to see another disciple of Tyler further dividing his attention.

"Okay. We're in the war room now, fellas," Tyler started his pre-game tirade. "This is Normandy. This is Stalingrad. This is the front lines. Defeat is not an option. It's kill or be killed. To victory!"

We each raised a drink as a toast and gulped them down.

"Tonight, we're going to be practicing what I call the *'long con'*. You've all had a taste of the one-night stand, but there will come a point in your career where you want something more, maybe a relationship, maybe not, maybe you'll want to have an ace in the hole you can pull out in case of an emergency. Maybe your game is off, maybe all the HBs are spoken for, maybe you're just feeling lazy, whatever. Here's where the long con comes in."

Darren and Rick leaned in closer to Tyler, desperate to hear what he was saying.

"What we're going to do tonight is divide up the club. We're each going to talk to..." He paused for a minute, looking out amongst the crowd, counting heads. "...two HBs, at least 7 or higher, for 5 minutes each, and then we're going to meet back here and debrief. You will not be going home with ANY of these women tonight. The idea is to reel them in and then break off, leave them wanting more. You set them up now and then reap the benefits later. Despite what you may think, being a pick-up artist isn't always about instant gratification. It takes a measure of self-control and discipline to become a master."

Darren scoffed and rolled his eyes. Rick just sat silently, soaking in his beloved master's wisdom.

"David, you're the guest, so I'm going to give you first dibs. Pick two women." He turned to Darren and Rick, "And no doubling up! I know you're all eager to prove who's top dog and shit but we're not there yet. Pick your own marks. Patience is a virtue."

"I'll take..." I looked out across the crowd, "the brunette, over by the bar, and... the blonde, taking to the DJ."

"Ooooh," Darren smirked. I turned, raising an eyebrow.

"A gutsy move, man," Tyler interjected, "That DJ is gonna be a hard AMOG to shut out, but I give you props."

"...AMOG?" I whispered to Tyler.

"Alpha Male Other Guy. The players. They aren't PUAs, but they're better than most of the sad sacks in here. DJs get into DJing for one reason and one reason only: the pussy."

"Who the fuck is this guy?" Darren muttered under his breath, clearly incensed that I hadn't done the necessary homework.

Tyler turned to him. "Alright, Darren, you're up."

"I've got the two brunettes on the dance floor." He ventured confidently.

Tyler narrowed his gaze, searching. "You better be talking about the two I'm looking at, 'cause all the other chicks out there are HB 5.5s at the most. Good eyes, though."

He turned to Rick. "Rick, what you got?"

"Uh... I'll take, the twins, at the table over there." Rick motioned across the club towards a pair of buxom blondes sitting at a booth. Two tall young men, dressed in expensive looking suits, sat across from them, laughing and gesturing wildly, though the girls seemed completely unamused by their posturing.

"God DAMN I love twins," Tyler laughed. "Who'd you think those guys are that are with 'em? Boyfriends?"

"No, not boyfriends." Rick said, quietly. "They're just hitting on them. They don't know they're *lesbians*."

Tyler burst into laughter. "Goddamn Rick, you make me proud."

Tyler stood up and shouted. "Go get 'em, boys! Back here in ten. If you can't close them in five you're dead to me. Names and numbers, people. Go, go, go!"

Rick and Darren leapt out of the seats and began snaking through the crowds towards their targets with a pinpoint accuracy. I slowly stood up and gave Tyler an incredulous look.

"Being a teacher is tough, but rewarding. Darren is a lost cause, but Rick...Rick is gonna do great things. I can't wait to see what he's capable of." There was a gleam of pride in his eye, like a father has for his sons.

"Really? He seems kind of squirrely to me."

"He may not look it but that guy is a *phenomenal* closer."

"Tyler... You are a disgusting, misogynistic pig." He raised an eyebrow as I continued, "But goddamn am I glad to have you as a friend."

"Stop, you're making me blush." He pushed me down the steps, urging me onwards. "Go get 'em, Tiger."

I smiled and shook my head, making my way through the crowd. I decided to go for the girl by the DJ first, might as well start with a bang.

As I approached the DJ table, the music slowly grew louder and louder until the underlying chatter became nearly inaudible. I slid up next to the blonde and listened in on the conversation she was having with the DJ.

"...yeah I've always thought that Deep Blue was their best album, but when I say that people look at me like I'm crazy!" Christ, she was one of those artsy types who thought every opinion they had was a unique snowflake. This was going to be tricky.

"It's definitely under-appreciated, but I've always thought their second CD was the best record they ever made."

She laughed and opened her mouth to reply, but I cut in. "Hey man, you got any Super Mash Brothers?" The DJ looked from me to her a few times, and then nodded. The girl turned to me.

"I LOVE the Super Mash Bros!"

"No way!" I replied, forcing myself to care, "I've been following them since they put out Fuck Bitches Get Euros in '04! Absolutely amazing shit. What's your favorite track?"

"God, do I have to pick one?!" She smiled and cocked her head, trying to decide. "I guess if I had to pick it'd be 'Still Bleeding' off All About The Scrillions."

"Excellent choice." I nodded to the DJ. "You heard the lady!"

He grumbled something under his breath and put the record on. The music came up and the girl started bobbing her head.

"Care to dance?" I offered her my hand. She smiled and took it, following me into the crowd.

We laughed and danced for a few minutes, and I looked out amongst the crowd, searching for the other students. My gaze caught Tyler, who was standing on the end of the bar, a beer in each hand, dancing to the music. He locked eyes with me and smirked, and then pointed to his wrist. I was running out of time.

I pulled the girl close and called out through the noise, "Hey, what's your name?"

"Sophie!"

"I'm David, nice to meet you!"

"No way! My ex's name is David!"

Fuck. That was going to be a hard one to come back from, and I just didn't have the time.

"Can I buy you a drink?"

"Sure! I'll have a Corona!"

I smiled and shook my head. Dirty Mexican beer. A woman after my own heart!"

She giggled and I gripped her hand softly before making my way to the bar. I'd come back with the beer after the brunette and subsequent debrief and she'd be none the wiser. I scanned the bar for the girl I had claimed earlier and saw her down at the back of the bar. Her back was to me, but compared to Sophie opening this girl should be easy as pie. I strode up to her as she was talking to a friend and put a hand on her shoulder.

"Hey! Have you--"

The girl turned and I was surprised to find it wasn't the same girl that I had noticed before. This chick was actually substantially more attractive than the one I had picked out. *Oh well, go with the flow.*

"I'm sorry; I thought you were someone else!" She eyed me quizzically for a minute, but I continued. "Have we met before? You look so familiar."

"I don't think so...?" she turned to her friend for a second and they giggled.

"Hrm. Must be fate then!" She smiled at me, kindly. Clearly she'd heard that line before. "What're you drinking? Next rounds on me."

She raised her empty shot glass. "Tequila."

"Perfect!" I motioned to the bartender for another round . "Three more shots! Oh, and a Corona please!"

I pocketed the Corona for later, and we raised our glasses in a toast, and after the fire water finished splashing around in my belly, I called out again.

"What's your name?"

"Nina."

"Hey, Nina. I'm David." She nodded, still somewhat skeptical. I was gonna have to throw a change-up into the mix.

"And who's your ravishing friend here?" I said, stepping past her, towards her friend. The friend was truly unfortunate looking, an HB 3 at best. She was a big girl, and didn't wear it well. Thick coke bottle glasses framed her perfectly round face which was turning beet red as I spoke to her.

She snorted as I approached. "I'm Debbie!"

"Well, Debbie, it's a pleasure to meet you."

I took her hand and planted a soft kiss on the back of her palm. She squealed in delight. Clearly, she didn't get much male attention.

"Such a gentleman," Nina interjected, seeming confused by my ploy.

This was called 'negging'. The idea was to run hot and cold with women, be nice to them, but then ignore them or criticize them on something small so that they know you know they aren't perfect. Most beautiful women are used to being put on a pedestal by men and idealized, few are used to being ignored or passed up, and they find that intriguing.

"And they say chivalry is dead," she continued, somewhat dryly.

"It's hard not to be chivalrous when you're surrounded by so many beautiful women!" I added, smiling wide. The music suddenly got louder as the tracks changed, and I knew this was an opportunity to be bold.

"So what do you do?" I called out to Nina over the noise.

"I'm an accountant."

I pretended I couldn't hear her. "A what?"

"ACCOUNTANT!" she yelled, louder.

I motioned to my ears and shrugged. She rolled her eyes and reached into her purse, pulling out a business card. I took it from her and read aloud, "Nina Showalter. Charted Accountant."

I nodded in understanding and pocketed the business card. I got what I wanted and time was almost up.

"Well, listen ladies, I gotta go check on my friend," I motioned to Tyler who was still at the end of the bar, dancing his ass off like a man possessed. "But it was great talking to you. Have a good night and enjoy the drinks!"

Nina and Debbie smiled at me, and I pushed back through the crowd to Tyler's table, where Rick was already waiting. I sat down across from him again and sized him up. He was staring down at his beer, grinning like a fool. Darren, however, was nowhere in sight.

Tyler leapt off the bar, and jogged back up to the table after spying our return in. "With a minute to spare! Way to go, guys." He looked around the club. "Where's Darren?"

Rick raised his head and spoke quietly. "He left with one of the brunettes. The tall one."

"Tina," Tyler shook his head and pulled up a chair at the head of the table. "Fucking amateur. I happen to know that girl has a Valtrex prescription at the pharmacy under the name butterfly. Hope he enjoys herpes." He regained his composure and turned to me.

"What you got for me, my man?"

"The DJ girl is Sophie. Didn't get her number, and not sure I want it. She's hot, but not that hot. She's one of those obnoxious artsy types. Loves music a little too much. Peeled her away from the DJ without too much trouble, though. He was looking at me like he was trying to get me to burst into flames with his mind."

"That was you with the Mash Bros, wasn't it?" He said, beaming.

"When I told her my name she freaked out; apparently her ex's name is David, too."

"Fuck, that's a bad beat right there. A good lesson to learn though: always have a backup name. Yeah, maybe your name's David, but you go by Dave for short. Or maybe your friends call you Hank because of this hilarious in-joke you have. *Don't let your name cockblock you.*"

I nodded, absorbing his wisdom. "Still, props for seeing it through. It takes a true artist to know when to cut his losses and move on. What about the brunette?"

"I lost her in the crowd, but picked a new target." I motioned down towards Nina and Debbie at the bar. They waved at me. "The cute one's Nina. Her not-so-cute friend's Debbie. Played up the friend a bit."

"And old but classic approach. Much respect. Did you get her number?"

I reached into my pocket and pulled out Nina's business card.

"Un-fucking-believable. This is what I'm talking about." He playfully punched me in my shoulder. "I think I've seen those two here before. We're gonna plant a seed here, buddy, and in time, it's going to grow into a beautiful fucking flower. And what do we do with the flower after it blossoms?"

He looked at me expectantly, and I shook my head. "Fuck it?"

Tyler exploded into riotous laughter for a few moments before turning to Rick.

"Rick," Tyler said, his voice conveying a sympathetic understanding. "Lay it on me. How bad was it?"

He smiled shyly, pulled a hand from lap and placed his fist on the table for us to examine. In the dim light of the club it was hard to make out, but we could see it was there; scrawled across the back of his hand in ball point-pen was a telephone number.

"Oh, hell no! Is that real?!" Tyler leapt up from his seat, in utter disbelief. "You did NOT. You did not just convert those smoking hot lesbians. Rick, what the fuck, man. *Who is this guy?!*"

Rick shrugged, grinning like a fool and I stared at the number in total shock. Rick turned towards the twins sitting across the bar, and they waved and blew kisses in his direction.

"They just haven't ever been with a real man," he said, bashfully, "They're sisters, from Norway."

Tyler threw his arms around Rick and kissed him on the top of his head. "Fucking legendary. This is what it's all about. Making the impossible work for you." Tyler took his seat again and ordered another round of shots.

"I'm proud of you guys. You stayed on task tonight and we're gonna make it pay off. But for now, we get fucked up and run the train on some bitches. But you, you stay away from that Nina girl. Give her time to let thoughts of you fester in her brain. And you, Rick, sweet Jesus man, go home. You've learned all I have to teach."

We raised our shot glasses and pounded one more round. I was pretty drunk at this point, but I knew it was too early to call it quits. The cold beer in my pocket urged back towards Sophie. I combed through the dance floor and found her once again.

"Hey!" I said, opening the beer with my shirt and handing it to her. "Sorry it took so long! It's impossible to get the bartender to notice you if you don't have a nice set of tits, you know?"

She laughed, "They do come in quite handy! I'm keeping my keys, wallet, and cell phone in mine as we speak!"

"No way in hell you got all that shit crammed up in them titties," I shouted, the drink doing most of the speaking for me at this point. One by one, she produced her personal effects from her cleavage, each item more shocking than the one preceding it.

"No effing way. Hey," I said, pulling her close. "You wanna get out of here?"

CHAPTER 8

It was a few months after our affair until the next time I heard from Anna. She had sent me a text message. Seeing her name across the screen of my phone pushed a lump into my throat.

">Hey, I know we're not really talking, but I'm having a birthday party next weekend. I know you hate parties, but I'd really love it if you came."

I knew she was asking mostly to be polite, and didn't think for a minute that I'd actually say yes. I had to prove to her that I had changed from the man she knew 5 years ago. This was new-David she was dealing with now, David 2.0, Super David.

">I'd love to." I replied, without hesitation.

">Haha, you shouldn't joke about stuff like that..." she replied, incredulously.

">Who's joking? And since when were we not talking?"

There was a pause before her next reply came. Clearly she didn't know what to make of me now.

">Well, great! I'll text you my address on Saturday. See you at 8!"

I smiled and closed my phone. I was on the path to greatness, I could feel it. This was the chance I was waiting for.

I arrived at her party a few minutes early, in the hopes that I could have a few minutes alone with her to work my magic before the other attendees arrived, but by the time I showed up it was clear the party was already in full swing.

I knocked on the door three times and waited, nervous tension welling up in my stomach. Fight or flight instincts began to take hold; it wasn't too late to turn around, leave, and forget this insanity. In truth, I was tired, so tired, of playing this insipid little game of cat and mouse, but I knew I had come too far to give up now. I was going to see this through until the end.

I heard footsteps creep up behind the door and fiddle with the door knob. Then, slowly, the door cracked open, and Anna's smiling face came into view.

"You made it," she said softly, a mixture of relief and disbelief coloring her words, and threw her arms around me.

"Wouldn't miss it for the world," I said, handing over her gifts. I bought her a bouquet of roses, and a CD, accompanied by a hand-written letter professing my love and admiration for her. "Happy birthday."

"You shouldn't have, David." She began to open the envelope, but I suddenly reconsidered.

"Save that for later. Read it after the party."

It is her birthday party; there was no reason to make her miserable and upset with my emotional garbage just yet. Let her have her fun. You're in no rush. You've waited five years for this, what's one more night?

She brought me inside and introduced me to her friends. I didn't recognize or know anyone there. As each stranger shook my hand and produced their names, I smiled and nodded. Some people seemed to know of me.

"Oh, you're David?" they'd say, "I've heard a lot about you."

I guess that was meant to comfort me, but it just made me paranoid. What had she told her friends about me? Was I going to be punished for the wrong-doings I had committed more than five years ago? I suddenly felt very much in danger, like I had fallen into the Lion's cage at the zoo. I was out of my element here, and no one would protect me.

After the introductions and pleasantries were dispensed with, I came to a realization. None of these people were Anna's new boyfriend; Nick was nowhere to be found. I later learned that night that Anna had dumped Nick, shortly after her night of debauchery with me. The breakup seemed to be based on other reasons, but I wasn't too interested in the why or how. All that mattered was that she was here, and she was single. This was my chance.

I stood on the wall and sipped my drink most of the night. I didn't have anything to talk to anyone about, and I really wasn't there to make friends. I was just there for her. I watched her bounce around the house, from friend to friend, laughing and talking and generally having a good time. She didn't seem to be in pain, like I was. She wasn't paralyzed by my absence the way I was by hers. She kept on living her life.

I watched her and her friends dance across the living room, various handsome men picking her up and spinning her around every alternate step. She was having a great time.

But I was dying inside. She didn't need me, I realized, the way I needed her. I looked at all these people she had collected over the years, to replace me, and realized they all gave her more than I ever could. I hurried to the kitchen and took a few shots of Vodka to push the sorrow from my mind.

Feeling my inhibitions vacate my mind, I decided I should accept defeat and throw in the towel before I ended up making a scene. I crawled up to her and tapped her on the shoulder. She turned to face me, a kind smile on her face.

"Having a good time?" She said.

"Yeah, yeah, it's great..." I lied to her, just like I always did. "But hey, listen, it's getting late so I think I'm gonna take off."

Distress spread across her face. "Are you sure?" she asked, giving me the opportunity to reconsider. "Are you okay to drive?"

I wasn't, really, but I'd much rather wrap my car around a telephone pole then spend another tortured minute watching her parade around the house without a care in the world, so I lied again. "Yeah, I'll be fine. Thanks for inviting me. Happy birthday."

She walked me to the door and I gave her one last nod before stepping out into the night.

I drove slowly, somewhat paranoid that I would get pulled over in my intoxicated state. It was late by the time I finally got home. I opened the door to my apartment and immediately fell onto the couch, finally giving myself permission to feel all the thoughts that tugged at my mind while I was at the party, and broke down, sobbing into the cushions with reckless abandon. I was sure it was over, this time. She was gone.

I cried for hours, until the sun came up, and I had finally become too exhausted to fight it anymore. I closed my eyes and drifted off to sleep.

The day after Anna's birthday party I woke up to the warm afternoon sun shining through shades which covered the sliding glass doors leading out to the balcony of my apartment. I rolled over and rubbed the sleep out my eyes. *How did I get home last night?*

I glanced at my phone to see what time it was but the screen was blank, so I reached over and pressed the power button on its face. No response. The battery must have died while I was out.

I clumsily picked myself off the couch and took the phone into my office to plug it into its charger. The drunken sleepfog still hadn't receded from my brain, my higher-brain functions still hadn't kicked back on, so I stood in my office, in the dark, and watched the battery indicator on the phone begin to slowly fill up for a few moments. Eventually, the digital clock read out returned to the screen. It was 2 in the afternoon.

Suddenly my fight or flight instincts kicked in and I ran into my bedroom, frantically pulling clothing out of the closet while simultaneously undressing myself. *My afternoon class started thirty minutes ago.* I bounded back down the staircase as I buttoned up my shirt and that's when I heard it: a familiar pinging noise from my phone that always sent a slight chill out of my spine. I cautiously approached my desk and snatched up the phone. A lump formed in my throat and checked the screen. One missed voice mail. *From Anna.*

What could it be about? What did she want? My heart began to pitter-patter as I launched into every possibility. Did she need me? Was she in trouble? The chemical and physiological precursors signaling the onset of a panic attack began to manifest: the cold sweats, the pupil dilation, the tremors.

Okay, calm down, I'm sure she's fine. Maybe she just wanted to talk.

Talk about what? How she realized how much she loved me? That she wanted to be with me after all? That she had spent every night for the past five years thinking about how great we'd be together, just I had? A sad smile crept across my face.

Or maybe she decided she didn't ever want to see me again. Either or.

After a few minutes of careful consideration, I finally worked up the courage to check my own voice mail.

There was a moment of hesitation before Anna's voice oozed through the speaker. I could hear the background noises of the party – still going strong at 3 AM, apparently – muffled by her heavy breathing.

"David..." she cooed after a moment, "David, its... its Anna."

Her words were slurred; it was clear that by this point in the evening she was quite drunk.

"I..." She hesitated again, clearly struggling to find the right way to phrase what she wanted to tell me. "I...I read your letter."

Another lump passed down my larynx as I suddenly recalled the most important gift I had given her last night. The gift of words, the love letter I had written for her, the letter I told her not to read until after I left. Maybe that was part of why I fled the party, I wanted her to read the note, I wanted her to know how I felt, even if I was too scared to face the consequences.

Anna sniffled, clearly holding back tears, "I...I'm going to come over to see you tonight. After I get off work. *I want to talk to you.*"

There was a hidden clause after her last sentence, a whole secondary string of thoughts that she had decided to leave unspoken. *What was it, Anna?*

What did you want to say to me? There were so many things we never said to each other throughout the years; so many words that we had convinced ourselves were better left unsaid. Somehow, we just couldn't let each other know how we felt. We were too scared the other would leave, because that's all we ever did to each other. We walked away. I walked away from her after she got out of the hospital, and she walked away from me when Nick came into her life. We were always in motion... Constantly changing footing, searching for higher ground, because we knew it was just a matter of time until the tide rolled back in and swept one of us away.

I wanted to tell her all these things, but somehow, I just...couldn't. So I wrote them instead. Anna had never written me anything over the years. There were no post scripts to her dialogue with me, everything was just as it seemed.

Not like me. I was a fraud, and I knew it. I had spent all these years trying to improve myself to impress her; I got a better hair cut, better clothes, took a little better care of myself, but all these superficialities could do nothing to cover up my core fundamental belief that at the end of the day...I was not worthy of her time or affections.

The phone message ended with the same awkward hesitation that had started it. I hung up the phone and moved back to the couch in the living room, letting my head fall gently against one of the pillows. I wasn't going to class today. I was going sit here, and wait for my destiny.

CHAPTER 9

I woke up to a tingling sensation in my arm. The morning light shone through the cracks of the curtains, casting a pale glow upon the woman crushing my arm. Sophie lay curled up next to me, her left hand resting on my shoulder. I watched her for a few moments and thought of how Anna used to look, sleeping in my arms.

I pondered trying to extract my numb limb out from beneath her and sneaking out for a few minutes before realizing that really, I didn't want to leave. It's true that Sophie and I had nothing in common, and on any other day I would have found her obnoxious pseudo-intellectualism completely off-putting, but on this particular morning, there was something comforting in the knowledge that I was somewhere, with someone, that under normal circumstances, I would not be. There was unfamiliarity here, the sense of adventure, of new destroying the old, and that maybe by sleeping with this girl, who was not at all like any I had been with before, I could find meaning in something other than the rock that I had based my entire adult life on: this idealized notion of 'the one'.

Lost in my thoughtful pondering I hadn't noticed Sophie stirring, the signs of life returning to her previously still form.

"Hey…" she murmured, as she bent over to kiss my cheek.

"Morning…" I replied softly.

I ran my forefinger across her exposed thigh, her milky white skin forming goosebumps in my finger's wake.

"What time is it…?" She cooed and nuzzled my neck as she closed her eyes once more.

I glanced across the bed and read the print out on the small digital clock on her nightstand aloud: "8:34."

Her eyes snapped open, her body becoming rigid and composed. "Shit!"

Sophie violently leapt out of bed, casting the bed sheets away as if they were a web of poisonous snakes, and began picking her clothes up off the floor. I admired her naked body for a few moments before snapping to attention. "Wh…what's wrong?"

"I was supposed to be at work a half an hour ago…"

She winced as she hoisted her panties up past her knees. Uncertain of what to do or say, I watched her as she ducked into the bathroom and hurriedly ran a hair brush through her locks with one hand while brushing her teeth with the other

I rallied, willing the hangover-induced cob webs out of my mind. We raced each other to finish dressing ourselves, but she was clearly a pro at getting ready under a state of duress. I was still fiddling with the zipper on my jeans when she exited the bathroom, looking even more radiant than she had the night before.

"I'm sorry, I've got to go… You can stay for a while if you want."

I pulled my shirt over my head and fished my jacket off the back off the bedpost.

"It's okay, I'll clear out too."

I didn't have anywhere to be, and I could use a few more hours of nap time, but a bad feeling, something like guilt or embarrassment, had crept into the pit of my stomach, and I knew it would only get worse the longer I stayed there.

Sophie and I walked down the stairs of her apartment building together in perfectly awkward silence, hesitating as we passed through the main door towards the front landing.

"I had great time last night," I said, smiling half-heartedly. I reached out and picked a piece of fuzz off her sweater. "I'll call you."

She smiled back and shook her head. "You don't have to lie to me, David. I'm okay with this being a one-time thing."

I chuckled and kissed her on the cheek. "Okay, now I'm *really* going to call you."

She nodded and started to walk off. "I hope that you do."

I watched her walk away, down the boulevard, until she became just a spec on the horizon. Then I called Tyler.

"We're losing sight of the goal."

"I take it it didn't go well last night with DJ girl?"

"No, it went great. *Too* great, in fact. I think I fell in love with her."

Tyler laughed. "You old romantic! So, you gonna see her again?"

"No," I stated plainly, "I'm not looking for new love; you're supposed to be helping me get Anna back."

"Patience, grasshopper. We planted the seeds, and now—"

"Yeah, yeah, I know, the fucking flower," I interrupted, getting somewhat frustrated at Tyler's useless metaphors. "What's our next move?"

"Well, I made some inquires," Tyler stated, taking a hushed tone like he was some sort super spy, "No one around seems to know much about this 'Nina' girl. She's new in town, moved here a few months ago for her job. She works at an accounting firm downtown."

I held the phone between my shoulder and ear, and began fishing around in my pockets for Nina's business card. I held it up and examined it, corroborating Tyler's story.

"Now, some of my associates claim she won't play ball, if you catch my meaning. This means one of two things; either she's frigid, or she's smart."

"I do like a challenge," I said, considering.

"I know you do," Tyler said, chuckling. "If we're gonna make this work, we're going to have to go undercover."

"Undercover?" I asked, uncertain if this was some sort of euphemism.

"Come over to my place tonight, and we'll figure out our game plan."

CHAPTER 10

"What are we *doing*?" Rick whispered from the backseat.

Tyler stared out over the dashboard through a pair of dark black binoculars he had purchased at an army surplus store not ten minutes before.

"We are *waiting* for Nina to leave her apartment, man! How many times have we gone over this?" Tyler scowled under his breath.

Rick nodded and settled back into his seat as Tyler continued to scan the boardwalk in front of Nina's apartment building.

"Sorry...." Rick whispered again.

"Why are we whispering?" I interjected.

Tyler pulled the binoculars away from his face and gave me a hard look. His eyes darted back and forth between me and Rick for a few seconds.

"I don't know. It seemed cool, man," Tyler said evenly as he shoved his face back into the lenses. "Why you always gotta ruin everything?"

"Oh, I'm sorry dude, I must have forgot the standard black ops protocol for stalking was to *loiter in a minivan* and *whisper*!" I replied, my patience for Tyler's stunts wearing thin.

"We ain't stalking nobody!" Tyler called back, "We're not gonna *follow* her when she leaves! Jesus, did anybody pay any fuckin' attention to the plan?"

"Maybe you should go over it again..." An unsteady nervousness in Rick's voice echoed my own sentiments.

Tyler sighed loudly and took a deep breath. "Okay. I called Nina's office, chatted up the receptionist and got her to give me Nina's home address. We are now sitting outside her apartment, and waiting for her to leave. When she DOES leave, we're going to break into her place and search for clues."

"Clues? What the hell is this, Nickelodeon? Clues to what?"

"I don't know! What she's into, if she's seeing somebody, whatever!"

"And we couldn't just ask her like normal human beings? You know, instead of committing a crime?"

Tyler rolled his eyes and shoved his face back into the binoculars. "Man, you don't know anything about women. You're lucky I'm so goddamn—"

Tyler's voice returned to a hushed whisper . "Wait, there she is!"

"What?"

"Nina! She's leaving her apartment!"

Tyler handed me the binoculars and pointed down the sidewalk. I looked through the lenses and saw her: Nina was walking down the steps from the doorway to her complex. She hesitated for a moment as she dug through her purse and after a brief struggle with its contents she produced her keys, which she then used to open the door to a car parked a few feet away. The three of us watched in silence as she pulled out of her parking spot and drove away. As soon as she was out of sight, Tyler sprung into action.

"Gentlemen. It's go time."

"Tyler, what if she comes back while we're up there?" I said, more and more doubt filling my mind with each passing second.

"That's where Rick comes in," Tyler replied as he reached into a black bag in the back seat. He produced a set of walkie-talkies and handed one to Rick before continuing. "Rick's gonna be look out. He sees her come back and gives us a shout over these bad boys so we have enough time to get out. You got it, buddy?"

Rick nodded and pressed his thumb against the broadcast button a few times in anticipation. "You can count on me."

"Tyler, I don't know about this..." I protested while pushing the passenger door open and stepping out onto the curb.

"Hey, relax man. Everything's gonna be fine." Tyler smiled at me out of the corner of his mouth as he came around the front of the car to join me. "Trust me."

We skulked up the stairs to the front door and I froze in my tracks.

"Tyler, you gotta be buzzed in..." I said simultaneously disheartened and relieved, motioning to the call box mounted on the wall to our right.

He shook his head and placed a heavy hand on the door handle. With a gentle tug it slid open, allowing us passage.

"After you, sir." He said, beaming with pride.

"What the...? How did you...?" I replied in utter disbelief as we stepped through the door way. As he eased it shut behind us, he pulled a small strip of electrical tape off the side of the door which was preventing the locking mechanism from sliding into place.

"I told you to trust me. I scoped the place out earlier, helped an old lady with her groceries." He grinned madly as he flicked the piece of tape to the floor.

"Ah, yes, Tyler the Good Samaritan, how could I have forgotten?"

He ignored my remark and raced up to the elevator which stood open, ready to take us higher into the complex. We boarded and Tyler began to fiddle with the control panel.

"Let's see... It was apartment 303."

Tyler pressed the button labeled '3' and a circular band of light illuminated the button. After a moment of violent shaking that nearly threw me to the ground, the elevator began to lurch skyward, toward the third floor.

"This is insane..." I mumbled under my breath as the LCD read out at the top of the elevator changed from '1' to '2'.

"Look, do you wanna bag this broad or not? You asked for my help with Anna, and I am giving it to you. If you don't like it, you're free to walk away."

I threw up my hands. "Alright, alright, already. I'm sorry. Don't get your panties in a twist."

Bing. The door opened and we stepped out onto the third floor landing. Tyler pressed a button on his walkie-talkie and began to speak quietly as he bobbed and weaved down the hallway, ducking behind corners and potted plants. I walked beside him at a brisk pace.

"How's it looking out there, Rick? Over."

For a moment there was no response. I immediately launched into a paranoid fantasy that Rick had somehow been caught and there would be no one to warn us of Nina's return. We were almost certainly fucked. But before the cold sweats could start, a brief beat of static echoed through the receiver, followed by Rick's timid voice.

"All clear. Over."

By the time Rick had gotten around to replying, we had reached unit 303.

"You didn't happen to help Nina with her groceries too, did you?" I remarked sarcastically as Tyler fiddled with the door knob to the apartment; it was locked. "Or perhaps you learned how to pick locks?"

"Always with the negativity, man."

Tyler took a step away from the door and bent down in front of the welcome mat, a concentrated look spreading across his face. His brow furrowed, and he looked around nervously for a moment before casting the mat aside. Underneath, there was a small iron ring with a single silver key attached to the hoop. Tyler replaced the mat and scooped up the keyring with his finger. He looked at me expectantly, but I was completely speechless. Even I was getting a little impressed by Tyler at this point.

"Okay, so what we looking for?" I asked, finally accepting that this was happening as Tyler pushed the door to Nina's apartment open and placed the key ring in the pocket of his hoodie.

"Anything that'll help us stack the deck." *Again with the stupid game metaphors.*

"Such as?" I looked a few steps forward and began to survey Nina's apartment.

It was surprisingly messy. Stacks of paper and folders crowded the living room table. Old magazines and newspapers spilled out from a file cabinet against the far wall.

"I don't know, man, you'll know when you see it." Tyler replied, the adrenaline clearly beginning to make him edgy. "I'll check the kitchen."

Tyler disappeared behind a pair of western-style double doors. I slowly moved across the carpet to the table to take a better look at the papers. I snatched the one on the top of the pile up and began to scan it for any useful information.

"Looks like work papers..." I thought aloud, completely unable to decipher any of the accountancy mumbo-jumbo that crowded the page in small evenly-spaced typeface.

Loud bangs and crashes began to come from beyond the kitchen divider as Tyler rooted around in her pantry. I pulled the top drawer of the metal file cabinet open and pulled out a stack of magazines. They were all medical journals...heavily dog eared too, it looked like she had gotten a lot of use out of them.

"I think she wanted to be a doctor..." I shouted across the room, hoping Tyler would be able to hear me above the ever increasing racket of pots and pans crashing against each other.

"What?" Tyler called out.

I sat down on the floor and spread the magazines out around me. I searched through the first one furtively for a few moments, before letting placing it back in place next to the others. Acting on instinct, I opened each magazine to the first marked page and found they all were related.

By this time, Tyler had emerged from the kitchen. "Nothing in there," he said, the squeaking of the saloon doors heralding his approach. "I mean it, nothing. Her refrigerator is practically empty. I guess she must go out a lot." He knelt down next to me as he realized I was deep in thought, "What'd you find?"

I sat in stunned silence for a moment and let the collage of articles do the talking. Circled, underlined, highlighted, they all were about one thing: cancer.

"You...you don't think...she...?" I mumbled, a sense of shame and dread entering my heart.

"Hmm," Tyler contemplated as he grabbed one of the magazines. It looked for the briefest of moments like he might actually be feeling empathy for another human being. I was wrong, as usual.

"This is good stuff, man. Maybe a family member died of cancer when she was a kid, or she knows someone with it now, I don't know. But we can make this work for us."

"Work for us...?" I said, shocked by his callousness.

"Yeah, man. She's clearly upset about it. Maybe she needs a shoulder to cry on."

I stood up, disgusted at Tyler and myself, but I decided not to say anything. Tyler was stuck in his ways, and if I insulted him anymore today he might reach his breaking point.

I scooped the magazines up and put them back into the drawer before easing it shut. Tyler had begun to snoop around the living room and had stopped at a bookcase by the door, eying a cluster of photographs on the shelf intently.

I walked up next to him and looked over his shoulder. There were several pictures of Nina with what must be her friends and co-workers, a few with an older couple that looked like they might have been her parents, but there was one photo that grabbed my attention.

The picture showed Nina in her graduation gown and cap, smiling widely as she tightly embraced a young man standing next to her. The man had green eyes and a shaved head, which made it difficult to determine his age. He looked at Nina with true affection in his eyes, something genuine and pure. It was very sweet.

Tyler scooped up a notebook from a desk by the door.

"Bingo! Found her day planner." He hunched over and began to page through the calendar. After a moment of frenzied page-turning he raised his fist, and shouted in success.

"Got it! She's gonna be at Club Armistice on Tuesday night. Guess where we're gonna be?" He turned to me expectantly and noticed my gloomy fixation on the photograph. "Oh no..." Tyler muttered as he followed my gaze. "Boyfriend?"

I shrugged casually and gave Tyler a look of indifference.

"Well," Tyler spoke confidently as he began striding towards the bedroom, "let's find out."

"Oh, come on Tyler, are we really going through her clothes?" I protested as he ripped the lid off her laundry hamper and began to rummage through the garments.

"This is beyond the pale..." I continued as he held up a tiny black thong. A mischievous smile spread over his face and I was sure he was going to pocket it, but after a moment he threw it back inside the container and put the lid back on.

"Nothing. Check the drawers." He motioned to a large oak dresser behind me. I pulled out each drawer, one after the other and awaited further instructions.

"Well?" Tyler called from inside the bathroom.

"Well *what*?" I called back, "There's nothing out of the ordinary here, just clothes."

"Girl clothes?" Tyler replied again, poking his head out from behind the doorway.

"Yes, of course girl clothes... What else would there be?"

"Good." Tyler said, "If that guy is her boyfriend, they're at least not serious. He'd at least left some of his clothes here. Looks like you're in the clear, my man."

"Well, that's a relief. Look Tyler, I don't think we're gonna find any—"

Suddenly, the piercing noise of static began to rumble from Tyler's pocket. It was Rick.

"Mayday, mayday!" Rick shouted. "The eagle has landed, I repeat the eagle has landed."

I didn't remember practicing any code words in the car, but I knew what Rick meant. Nina was back. Tyler and I exchanged worried glances for a moment and then raced back into the living room.

We burst out the door, back into the hallway, towards the elevator. Tyler pressed the call button frantically and we watched the LCD display with trepidation as the elevator slowly trundled up from the ground floor.

"Come on, come on..." Tyler whispered, nervously jingling the contents in his pocket. Suddenly a look of horror came over his face. He pulled his hand out slowly, and looked at me.

"The key...!" He whispered.

He darted back towards the apartment and dove onto the mat, sticking the keys underneath in one deft motion. He rolled onto his back and flipped back onto his feet like some sort of ninja and raced back to the elevator, returning just as the doors opened.

Sweaty and out of breath, Tyler and I moved to enter the elevator, but found our path was blocked by someone trying to exit it. A young woman brushed past us quickly, fumbling with several brown paper grocery bags, which looked full to the point of bursting. Her face was covered by her purchases, but I knew in my heart, it was her. *It was Nina.*

We filed into the elevator and I tapped the lobby button as quickly as I could. I was watching Nina walk down the hallway towards the door to her apartment that we had just broken into not 30 minutes ago. Just as the elevator doors began to close, she dropped one of the bags and bent over to pick it up. Then her eyes caught mine for the briefest of moments before the doors slammed shut.

"Shit...!" I whispered to Tyler. "What's wrong?"

"That's was her...!

"...What?"

"That was Nina! I think she saw me...!"

"Holy shit..." Tyler's eyes grew wide, though not from fear, but...joy? "That's epic! It's like we're in a spy movie, dude. This is awesome!"

I rolled my eyes and gave him a hard look.

"Well, I'm glad you're having so much fun, Tyler! Let's just get the fuck out of here..."

CHAPTER 11

"Okay, now we're stalking her." I muttered as I glanced out the car window, watching the lights from all the flashing neon signs zoom by as we speeded on into the night.

"It's only stalking if she knows we're following her. This will just be...a happy coincidence."

Tyler was truly gifted at spinning any bad situation into something positive. In another life, he would have been a great marketing executive. In a way, that's what he did: market himself to women, convince them that they needed him.

We pulled up to Club Armistice around ten-thirty. Tyler had decided it was better to be fashionably late whenever he went 'gaming', there was a better chance the women would be intoxicated and therefore it would be more easily seduced by his wiles. We entered the club and I began looking around for Nina.

"There she is," Tyler nodded toward to a booth at the far end.

I steeled myself and took a step forward, ready to play Tyler's stupid game when all of a sudden he threw his arm across my chest and held me back.

"Not so fast there, champ. This is going to call for extreme measures."

"What are you talking about?"

"We already know she's not gonna fall for the little league stuff. She's a new girl in a big city, her anti-slut defense systems are at maximum power. We're gonna have to lower her shields first."

"...and how exactly are we going to do that, Tyler?"

He turned to face me and nodded back over his shoulder. A group of loud, bubbly women giggled and shouted from a booth just a few feet away. I eyed a few of them for a moment. They were pretty, sure, but they had nothing on--

"No, don't look at them! Jesus, man..." He said, shoving my shoulder slightly to regain my attention. "Alright, look. What we're gonna do here is start a jealousy plot line."

"A *what*?" Tyler sensed my hesitation and instantly found a rationalization that was custom tailored to my sensibilities.

"Think of it this way, man. We're writing our destinies here. And in every good story, there's a plot twist."

I stood there, mouth agape as I considered his proposal. After a few moments of inner turmoil, I gave in.

"Okay..." I answered after taking a deep breath. "What's the plan?"

"Since you've already got your mark, I'm gonna open this group. You're gonna be *my* wingman tonight."

I nodded, somewhat eager to see the master at work. "What do I do?"

"Go over and stand by the bar, close to Nina, but don't let her know that you know she's there. Order some drinks or something. I'll give you the signal in a minute."

"The signal...?"

"Just go with it, man."

I summoned some courage and headed over to the far side of the bar by Nina's booth, careful not to look directly at her. I let my elbows rest on the edge of the bar as I tried to get the bartender's attention. I had been careful to keep Nina out of my line of sight, but I may have done too well – watching her out of the corner of my eye, it seemed like she hadn't even noticed my presence. It was time to do something drastic.

A woman to standing a few feet down the bar from me had just gotten her drinks and was about to turn around to head back to her table. I hustled up to her and stood behind her, and as she turned into me her drinks went crashing to the floor with a loud smash. The entire club seemed to hush for the briefest of moments, as if to mourn the lost booze.

"Oh my god, I'm so sorry!" she cried, clearly embarrassed.

"Don't worry about it," I smiled, "Let me buy you another." I motioned to the bartender. "Get the lady a new drink. Make it two."

He nodded and poured two new glasses and handed them to me, and I passed one along to her.

"Thank you so much... I'm Christie." The woman offered politely as we clinked our glasses together.

"*David.*" I said it loudly enough to make sure Nina would be able to hear me. Out of the corner of my periphery I was almost certain I could see her head turn.

"DAVID!" My call echoed back.

I looked across the bar towards the entrance and saw Tyler gesturing at me wildly. I nodded and began to head over. As I approached the table he was sitting at with two beautiful women on each side of him, I began to hear fragments of their 'conversation'.

"...and then when we got back to the hotel, it turned out the stripper was a guy! You shoulda seen the look on Mark's face!"

The girls burst into riotous laughter and Tyler leaned back, a knowing smile creeping across his face. He soaked in the attention for a few minutes before acknowledging.

"Hey, there he is," Tyler said, standing up boisterously. "Ladies, this is David. David is the smartest guy I know."

What he said was a blatant lie, I knew, but I understood what has happening. He was playing me up, and now I was expected to reciprocate; and endless social proof-building feedback loop. Classic play when two guys are gaming a set.

The ladies smiled coyly and blushed as I took a seat next to them. "Good evening, ladies."

"I was just telling them about Mark's bachelor party."

There was no Mark. Tyler didn't have any friends named Mark. Tyler didn't know anybody named Mark. Tyler lived in a Mark-less universe.

"Oh, man, that night was crazy," I replied, playing along. "You sure do know how to throw a party, Tyler."

"What can I say? *I just love making people happy.*"

There was a cold aloofness in his voice, but he wasn't lying. Tyler got off on giving people something to do, something to make them feel alive. Sure, I resented Tyler for a lot of the ridiculous things he'd put me through, but I knew in my heart that everything he did was because he wanted to help me. That's why we were here, tonight, running the train on these drunken bimbos – *because I needed his help.*

Tyler started motioning across the room with his eyes, towards the dance floor.

"Would you ladies care to dance?" I said, catching onto his cue. I extended a hand to the girl closest to me as I stood up, and Tyler and I lead them down past the bar, towards the back of the club where it wasn't so crowded. Where Nina would be able to see us.

The four of us danced for a few minutes, until Tyler excused himself to buy us another round of drinks. Liberal application of alcohol was frowned on by some more elitist players, but Tyler knew there was no use in denying yourself a useful tool simply in the name of ethics. All's fair in love and war, as they say.

"Your friend seems really nice," the girl Tyler had been dancing with called out to me.

"Yeah, Tyler's a great guy," I replied, "He's my best friend. I'd take a bullet for him."

"That's so sweet," the other one chimed in. She lowered her voice and leaned over to her friend, but she was clearly too drunk to be able to adequately modulate the volume of her own voice. "This guy is really cute..."

They giggled and I smiled, pretending not to hear their 'secret'. Tyler returned with four shot glasses and we each downed our drink in rapid succession. Suddenly, the dance music changed to a slow song.

"I pulled some strings with the DJ," Tyler said, clearly detecting our confusion. "Shall we?"

He pulled the first girl close to him and began to gently rock her back and forth in his arms. I rolled my eyes at him and followed suit.

I wrapped my arms around her waist – this girl whose name I didn't even know – and swayed back and forth for a few moments. She placed her head on my shoulder and followed my lead clumsily – clearly the drink was not sitting well with her.

After a few minutes she looked up at me and said, "You have really beautiful eyes."

"Thank you," I replied.

She leaned in close, and it looked like she was going to kiss me, but suddenly a look of distress came over her face and she pulled away. Placing her hands over her mouth she turned and began sprinting towards the bathroom. *Great. How romantic.*

I went to follow her, but realizing I couldn't enter the ladies room, I propped myself up against the wall by the door and closed my eyes, trying to figure out how I was going to salvage the situation. Suddenly, a voice broke into my thoughts.

"Haven't we met somewhere before?"

I opened my eyes and saw Nina emerging from the bathroom. She was smiling.

"Oh, h-hey...!" I stammered, taking completely by surprise. "N-nina, right? How are you?"

"Better than your friend, I think. Sounded like she had a bit too much to drink tonight, eh? That wouldn't be your doing, would it?"

I smiled, and shook my head. "Now why would you think something like that?"

She nodded and started walking back to her booth, so I followed alongside her.

"So...can I buy you a drink?" Nina laughed and kept walking. She sat down at her booth, and I sat down across from her.

"I'm fine, thank you."

I nodded solemnly and looked around the club. "So, you're here alone tonight?"

"Unfortunately, yes. Got stood up by a date, actually."

"Well, I guess I lucked out then," I quipped back. "Lucky for you I don't mind being your second choice."

"Oh, so you're my consolation prize? How grand." She laughed and sipped her drink. "You know, it's funny, I actually thought about you the other day. I *swore* I saw someone who looked just like you at my apartment building."

Ulp. "No kidding...? Must be fate then." I froze for a moment as I realized I had already used the 'fate' line on her once before.

"Do you really believe in fate?" she said, leaning forward, "Or is that just a line you use to pick up women?"

I chuckled, playing it cool. "As a matter of fact, I'm very spiritual. Here, give me your hand." She eyed me suspiciously for a moment and then extended her forearm across the table.

"Ever had a palm reading?" I asked furtively. She shook her head and bit her lip. *Got her.*

The palm reading trick was an essential utility in the pick-up artist's arsenal. It did two things: allowed for subtle 'cold reading'-type suggestion for girls who were inclined to believe in that sort of superstition, and it was a terrific compliance test; a check to see the woman's willingness to be physically touched by you.

I traced the lines on her palm with the forefinger of my right hand while holding it firmly with my left. Her hand was soft, like silk, and so very warm. I felt something familiar as I grazed her fingertips with the side of my palm. There was safety in her touch; I could imagine her fingers intertwined with mine, or gliding down the sides of my face to comfort me. I wasn't sure what this sensation was that I was experiencing, but I decided to push it from my mind for the moment.

"Ah, yes..." I said, pretending to channel some sort of cosmic energy. "You see this line? This is your life line. It's nice and healthy, extends all the way down to the base of your palm, so that means you're going to live a good long life."

She looked at me sadly as I spoke. For some reason I thought of all those articles about cancer Tyler and I had found in her apartment.

"and...and this," I continued, trying not to lose focus, "is your love line. See how it's kind of bisected by these other two lines? That indicates that you've had one...no, two great loves, with a third coming up soon."

In truth, I didn't know a goddamn thing about palm reading. But it didn't matter, as long as the woman didn't either. Just tell them something good, something that will make them excited.

She withdrew her palm and smiled, "Very impressive, David."

She remembered my name?

Just then, the girl I had been dancing with earlier burst out of the bathroom, covered in her own puke and sobbing loudly, crying out for her friend. Tyler and the other girl ran over to console her, and I knew it was time to be bold.

"Hey..." I whispered to Nina, "You wanna get out of here?"

For a moment, I wasn't sure if she would accept my invitation. My gaze flitted anxiously between her and Tyler, who I could tell out of the corner of my gaze was searching for me, most likely to shift the responsibility of caring for the sick girl onto someone else so that he could take her friend home. I probably owed Tyler that much, after all he had done for me, but as I looked at Nina I knew there were bigger things at stake here. Tyler was a good guy, he would understand.

Nina seemed to consider things for a moment before grabbing her purse and standing up. "Let's go."

CHAPTER 12

"So what's your story?" I asked, handing Nina her low-fat mocha.

We had stopped at a café a few blocks over from the club. It was one of those super-indie type joints where teenagers would go and listen to their iPods and talk about bands no one had ever heard of with aspiring authors who were pretending to work on their novels waited for someone to make conversation with them. The whole scene sort of bummed me out but they made pretty damn good coffee as long as you didn't offend the sensibilities of the baristas, who were always young, disenfranchised punks covered in tribal tattoos and all manner of piercings indicating the lack of a strong parental figure in their life.

"What do you mean?" Nina replied, smiling kindly as she blew on her drink to cool it down.

"You know, where are you from, what's your family like, all that kind of stuff?"

"Do you really want to know? Or do you just think I won't sleep with someone until they've memorized my biography?"

I laughed. *Damn, she's good.*

"You wound me, madam! I really want to know!"

"Well," she sighed, "I was born in Seattle. I went to college at Gonzaga University in Spokane where I got my degree. I got offered a job out here earlier this year and moved down a few months ago."

"What about your childhood?"

"Oh, you know, same old same old. We lived in a modest house in a good neighborhood in the suburbs. My dad is a dentist and my mom is a school teacher. We weren't wealthy by any means, but we did alright. I went to a catholic grade school because my parents thought I'd get a better education at a private school than a public one. Really, I think it just made me extremely cynical."

"Cynical? So, you're not down with the whole 'God' thing?"

She shrugged. "There might be a God, but if there is I don't think he cares what we think about him. I'm a realist, I try to only deal in things I can see and touch and feel. Things that are measurable. Things we can objectively know to be true or false. If God gave us intellect and reason, I don't think he meant for us to forgo their use. I don't think anyone can know for sure if there is a God or not, images of the Virgin Mary appearing on pieces of toast notwithstanding."

I laughed. "So what about Pascal's wager? I mean, don't you think it's better to believe and be wrong than not believe and be damned to hell for all eternity?"

"Pascal? Nice name drop." She smirked, but I think she was really impressed. "I try to live a good life based on my own morals. I do good things because I want to, not because I fear divine comeuppance in the afterlife."

Wow. A woman after my own heart.

"So what made you so cynical?"

"Besides the beatings from the nuns?" She chuckled, and reached into her purse. She pulled out her wallet and fumbled with it for a few moments before pulling something out and passing it across the table to me. I unfolded it slowly. It was a picture. In the photo of I could see her, Nina, hugging a man who looked a few years younger than her. The guy's face looked very familiar to me, but I couldn't quite place him...

"That's my brother, Rex," Nina continued, her voice starting to sound shakey. "That photo was taken last year. 6 months ago he was diagnosed with pancreatic cancer."

My eyes widened as I recognized the man; he was the guy who was in the picture of her apartment. He didn't have any hair in that picture, so I didn't recognize him before, but now... Oh god, all the medical journals...it all makes sense.

"When I was young I used to believe that God had a plan for me, that everything happened for a reason...then when we found out about Rex, I...I tried to understand the reason...What greater good could possible come out of it, but...eventually I realized, it didn't matter. There wasn't any reason in the world that would make losing my baby brother okay..."

"I'm so sorry, Nina," I said, looking up at her. "I didn't know..."

She frowned, clearly fighting off tears and took the picture out of my hands, stroking it fondly for a few seconds before stuffing it back into her bag.

"How long does he have...?" I said softly, trying to be delicate in my phrasing.

She shook her head. "Could be years, could be weeks... It's hard to tell with this stuff... We've tried all sorts of treatment, but nothing really seems to be working..."

I nodded and gently put a hand on her arm. "My dad died of lung cancer when I was young. I know how hard it is. The important thing is that you don't give up hope."

She looked into my eyes, searching for something. An agenda, an angle, something to explain my sympathy, but she found nothing. I was speaking from the heart, from experience.

"The human body is amazingly resilient. It can do amazing things. You just have to believe, you have to make sure Rex doesn't stop fighting. The minute he loses the will to go on is when it becomes too late."

She wiped a tear from her cheek and nodded. "Thank you, David..."

I smiled softly and nodded back. She took a minute and composed herself before speaking again.

"So enough about my sob story... Tell me about you."

"Well, there's not much to tell... I've lived here my whole life. My mom died giving birth to me, and well, when Dad got the cancer diagnosis I think he didn't have any more fight left in him. He died when I was 10."

"I'm so sorry..."

"It's okay. I lived with my Aunt and Uncle for a few years, and then they moved across the country so I started living with my grandmother until I graduated High School. I worked for a while to help Nana to pay the bills and eventually saved up to move out and start taking classes at a community college."

"What are you studying?"

"Political science and psychology, mostly."

"That's really cool, David. Are you thinking of a career?"

I shook my head, "No, not really... I just like learning about how people think. My first love has always been language."

"So you like books?"

"Not really," I smiled, "but I love writing. Ever since I was a kid I loved to write stories about stupid little things that made me happy."

"Like what?"

"Oh, I don't know... Like, in sixth grade we had some guest speaker come in and make us put on plays about how to save the environment or something. My friends didn't know what to write it about and so I ended up doing everything and writing this long play about the country running out of energy and so the President goes to go visit an Amish community and they teach him the secrets of living without electricity.

It was actually pretty funny. We dressed up in fake beards and everything. I think we kind of missed the point entirely, but we had a good time."

Nina giggled, "That's sounds awesome. What sorts of things do you write now?"

"I don't know... Your average thinly-veiled autobiographical fables disguised as fiction. I have dreams of writing the next great American novel, but every time I try I get stuck. Can never think of how to end them."

"Writer's block?" She mused.

"No, it's different than that... It's like there's something stopping me. Like I don't want the story to end. Real-life doesn't have endings, you know? Nothing ever *ends*."

"Don't your characters ever find happiness, though? You know, become a better person, live a better life, fall in love?"

Even if they did, that's still not 'the end'... Relationships are never finished, just abandoned.

I shook my head. "I guess that's the hard part for me. Figuring out what it would take to make them happy. That's always been my problem. *I've never been very good at helping people.*"

"I don't believe that for a second..." She smiled softly and touched my hand. We shared a brief moment of human connection, before she withdrew it and placed it back in her lap.

"So," Nina continued, clearing her throat as she ran a delicate hand through her silky hair, "Where did you and Tyler meet? Seems like you two get along well."

"Yeah, yeah," I stuttered for a minute before snapping back to reality, "Tyler's a really good guy, and a great friend. We actually met at college, in a cooking class of all things."

"I have a hard time imaging Tyler with an apron and oven mitts."

I snorted, "Yeah, well, you know, he was taking the class because he thought it would improve his 'game'. You know, ladies love a man who can cook for them and all that. I was taking it because I was tired of eating instant noodles every night for dinner. He was my cooking partner, and I guess we sort of hit it off. To be honest, for a long time I thought he was really shallow and obnoxious, but...he never gave up on me. He always was there, trying to be my friend. I was never really sure if he thought was a legitimately interesting person, or he just took pity on me."

"Why would he pity you?"

"I don't know. I mean, you've heard my story, I'm not exactly living the golden life. Tyler's had everything in his life so easy, I don't think he understands how people can be unhappy in their circumstance. He's always tried to make me rise above my station, but that's easy to say when you're devilishly handsome and and fill your personal swimming pool with wads of money."

"Tyler's rich?"

"Yeah, yeah, his parents were investment bankers or something. They left him a lot of money when they died. He's basically been riding off his inheritance his whole life. Never done an honest day's work as long as I've known him."

"Oh, god. How did his parents die?"

"They were both in an airplane crash on the way to some big industry conference in Europe. Life insurance paid off triple since they died on a business trip." I smiled grimly. "I guess Tyler always saw a little of himself in me, that if things had just been a little different, he might be the starving artist living in the inner city and I'd be the cool friend with beautiful women at my every beck and call."

"He does seem to have a way with romance..." Nina said, almost begrudgingly. She seemed almost upset that as an ambassador of woman-kind she was forced to cede that the majority of her gender were reduced to naught but giggles and coy blushing around Tyler.

"You don't even know the half of it. It is insane what he gets away with sometimes. He's got attracting beautiful women down to a science. He's actually been trying to teach me a few of his tricks."

She raised an eyebrow and I suddenly remembered who I was talking to. "And how's that working out for you?"

I swallowed and mustered a smile. "Well, you're here, aren't you?" She opened her mouth to responded but I quickly qualified. "Though, I don't think the reason you're here has anything to do with Tyler, does it?"

"You never know, maybe I'm just using you to get closer to Tyler. Maybe I'm trying to make him *jealous*."

I blinked a few times, uncertain if she was pulling my leg or if she had caught onto our scheme. I decided to play it cool.

"Well, I hate to break it to you, but Tyler is immune to jealousy. It's gonna take a lot more than that to throw him off."

"Maybe I'll just have to step it up a notch then," she said, standing up from the table. "Take me to dinner tomorrow night?"

My eyes widened as I realized she was serious.

"I'd love to. Anything to help a *friend*."

Even though it was clear that Tyler's playbook wasn't going to work on this girl, I found myself automatically coughing up his canned responses. Making it clear that you just want to be friends can often throw women into an existential confusion. *Why doesn't he want to sleep with me? Am I not good enough for him?* Even beautiful girls can be reduced to rubble if you know how to pick at those kind of nagging insecurities.

She pulled a pen from her purse and began scribbling on a napkin for a few moments. I snatched it up perhaps a little too eagerly after she slid it across the table.

"Pick me up at 8. Here's my address," she said, "I don't think you'll have any trouble finding it." A bead of sweat trickled down my neck and I laughed nervously.

"O-okay! See you at 8! G-goodnight!" I called after her as she began to make her way to the exit of the cafe.

"Good night, David."

I pulled out my phone to call Tyler so I could tell him the good news, but as my hand hovered over the call button, I reconsidered. Any progress I had made tonight, any ground that I had gained, was through my own effort and ability, not the product of any of Tyler's schemes. The 'jealousy' angle hadn't panned out, and he was probably mad at me for ditching him when things went bad. No doubt he would tell me to flake out on my date with Nina, make it look like I was busy or aloof or something, but I wasn't prepared to let the success of this stage of the plan ride on Tyler's idea of love We had passed the hook-up phase and entered the realm of romance and emotional connection, things which he simply knew nothing about.

I'm on my own from here.

CHAPTER 13

Anna didn't get off work until 2 AM on weekdays, but I stayed up all night waiting for her. I couldn't bring myself to do anything but sit and contemplate what she would say when she eventually arrived. Was she mad at me? Was she happy? What would be the outcome of the night's proceedings? I couldn't shake the notion that my entire life was balanced on a razor's edge. Whatever happened between us on that night would decide the rest of my life. How can you prepare yourself for something like that?

After what seemed an eternity of patient waiting, there was a knock at my door. My heart leapt into my throat and I knew that there was no going back now. Whatever would happen would happen, and I had no choice but to let the chips fall where they may.

I took a deep breath and pulled the door open, and welcomed her into my home without a word. Anna and I stood there for a few moments in silence as we each searched for the words to express ourselves.

"How...are you?" I started, deciding it was best ease into things.

She rejected my invitation to engage in self-deception, to pretend that this meeting was a simply pleasantry and not the harrowing moment of revelation and truth that it would eventually turn out to be, and threw her arms around me, gripping me tightly.

"I've missed you..." She whispered into my neck. "I've...missed you too, Anna. Every day of my life." We collapsed onto the couch together, refusing to let go of each other.

"I need you in my life, David..." she continued, the drama in her voice increasing with every word. "You're too important for me not be with, but... I'm scared. I'm scared that if we mess this up again then I'll have to go the rest of my life not having you with me."

"I understand exactly what you mean, Anna. Everything is riding on this..." That was an understatement. Everything wasn't 'riding' on this, in point of fact, this – me and her together – was everything.

"What do you want, David...?" She looked up into my eyes as she spoke, searching for a deep meaning. She knew me well enough to know that whatever I would say wouldn't be a hundred percent true and that she would need to watch my eyes – the windows to my soul – to piece together the whole story.

Something collapsed inside of me as I considered her question. A dam in my mind which had been carefully constructed over the years to hold back the torrent of emotion sprung a leak as I looked into her eyes, and in a matter of moments, pure unfiltered truth began to spill forth from my lips in ever increasing velocity.

"I want..." I started to speak, the quivering in my lips and vocal tonality belying the violent undercurrent of the raging tempest in my mind.

How many of my sentences to her start with the definite article, anyway? I — always I — and never *her*. I never knew what she wanted, or how to give it to her, and here I was trying to convince her that time had healed all wounds and given me enough wisdom to fix what my own hands had once made broken.

"I want you... I want to live with me, here, in this crappy apartment, and I want to come home from work every day and you say to me 'hi baby, how was your day?' and then I tell you all about the hard work I did that day, pouring over the minutiae of the Stevenson account, but that even though it was tough work, soul-crushing work even, I did it to support our family, to sustain the life until I was dead and buried in the cold earth, if it only meant that you would be happy and comfortable."

Anna's eyes widened and tears began to form at the corners of her eyes. I continued my rant, my voice growing higher and faster with each word.

"And then I want to have dinner and drink a bottle of wine with you before going up to bed and climbing underneath the sheets with something to read — maybe I'd read the day's issues of the Times, maybe you'd be reading Cosmo — and in the silence of our contemplation we would lie together in bed, you resting in the crook of my arm and then we would discuss and debate the issues of the day with vigor and passion, and then…and then we would make love, just as we had the previous night, and every night before it, and it would be somehow even better than all those times, but not as good as tomorrow, and then lying awake in the dead of night, our sweaty glistening bodies breathing heavily under the moonlight you would break the beautiful silence and say 'I love you, David Fox. I always have and I always will,' and then I'd say back to you 'I love you too, Annabelle Roberts. Now and forever,' and then our hands would find each other underneath the sheets and we will drift off to sleep, the last conscious thought passing through our minds being that this, this thing that was between us that some might describe as love, would be there waiting for us tomorrow, and we could rest safely in the knowledge that it was perfect and would never ever go away."

I swallowed hard and gasped for air, my elevating heart beat growing ever louder in my chest. I felt dizzy from the torrent of honesty, and was scared out of my mind that because of what I had shared with her she would realize what I had tried to hide from her all these years: that I really and truly was *out of my fucking mind*.

But instead, she just smiled sadly and took my hand in hers and said the most perfect thing I could have ever dreamed of.

"I want all that too, David…" I pulled her close, trembling in some sort of bizarre dichotomy of disbelief and joy. "I want all that too."

We held each other and talked until the sun came up, but nothing we could say to each other could really match what had come before: the realization that we wanted each other, that we wanted our lives to fundamentally converge and become a singular entity that would transcend our flimsy mortal flesh.

We spoke of the past and what we would do this time to 'make things work', negotiating the terms of our 'getting back together'. We were each quick to make concessions and empty promises of 'how things would be', which really, in the end, all amounted to nothing more than fanciful, delusional variations of 'let's try again…but this time it'll work!' and 'I still hate you, but you're comfortable and familiar so I'm willing to settle'.

But we did back together, and for a while it was great. Those blissful days during the initial 'honeymoon period' of our reunion were some of the happiest days of my life. There was a sense during that time that I finally passed a threshold, overcame an obstacle in my life that had loomed over me for years, restricting my forward motion through life. I had been pushing this boulder up a mountain for as long as I could remember, with no end in sight, and, finally, I had found even ground on which to rest, where I was no longer forced to push against my own circumstance or be crushed by gravity's indifference.

We went out and spent endless romantic nights together. The sex was better than it ever had been, a far cry from the awkward gropes and whispered apologies that made up my 'technique' back when I was a teenager. There was a totality behind everything that seemed to be pointing to an outcome that we both desired: that things were different this time. That we would work.

Looking back, I think that things were different for us for a while, but something happened. Over time, we found ourselves revisiting familiar scenes from a previous act, picking up where our narrative had left off. The endless nights and countless fights slowly crept back into the relationship, once again turning us into the people we hated to be, trapping us in a history we ourselves had written, and despite it all, we were always, in the end, doomed to repeat it.

CHAPTER 14

I left for Nina's early the next day, deciding that punctuality, no matter how boring it may be, was safer than risking her scorn if I was fashionably late. I still hadn't figured Nina out, and Tyler was being no help at all, so I didn't even call him to let him know what was happening. I didn't need any more of his misogynistic propaganda polluting my thoughts. Tonight, I was just going to be myself.

Apprehensively, I pressed the buzzer on the intercom by the doorway. It rang for a few moments and I busied myself trying to fix my hair with my distorted reflection in the chrome plating on the box.

"Hello?" her voice came through, scratchy and static.

"Hey, it's me." I called back. "David."

"Oh, you're early. I thought it might be the *other* guy I was going on a date with tonight. Oh well, come on up." She chuckled slightly and hit the buzzer. The door before me unlocked with a loud clunk. No electrical tape was gumming up the works today.

I pulled the door open and made my way into the lobby. Entering the elevator, I braced myself for its unstable shuddering, but this time it seemed to glide effortlessly up the rails, like somehow it knew that this time, I was supposed to be there.

I walked up Nina's door and remembered the anxiety I felt when Tyler and I were there just a few days ago. Compared to committing felonies, this was nothing. I entered state just as I knocked on her door. There were crashes and bangs as she scrambled up to the door and after a brief hesitation she slowly pulled it open.

"Hey David. Sorry, I'm not quite ready yet, but come on in and make yourself at home."

I stepped across the threshold into her home, and handed her a bouquet of roses I had picked up on my way over, at a corner store just a few blocks from her apartment. It was a totally spontaneous, happenstance act – I hadn't even thought about it until I noticed the flowers in the storefront window – but she would think I had it planned out the whole time.

"Flowers? For *me*?" She seemed a little incredulous as she took the roses from me. She smiled slightly and sniffed them before speaking again. "They're lovely, David. Thank you. I'll put them in water."

She disappeared behind the double doors into the kitchen and began speaking over the divider to me as she filled a vase with water from the sink.

"You know, I didn't really have you pegged for a flower-giving kind of guy."

Never stop surprising women, always defy their expectations and be perfectly unpredictable. Familiarity breeds contempt.

"Is that so? " I called back, "I'll have you know I can be very romantic when I want to be."

She smiled as she passed by me on her way back to the bedroom. "I never would have guessed. Have a seat." She gestured to the couch and I took a load off.

There was a moment of silence as I tried to decide on my next course of action. "You've got a great place," I said, feigning surprise by all of the things I had seen already. "You don't have to lie, it's a mess. Truth be told I don't get many gentleman callers coming up here."

"Oh, really?" I replied. "Why do I find that hard to believe?"

There was a moment of hesitation before she replied. "...What exactly are you implying?"

"I'm just saying, a beautiful young lady like yourself and no swarms of suitors vying for your affection? That's difficult to imagine. Are you a secret serial killer or something?"

"Well, I'm not saying they didn't try to get in here," she replied smugly, re-emerging from the bathroom with all manner of curlers and other contraptions I couldn't identify tangled in her hair. She reached into her purse which was sitting on the end table next to the couch and removed her lipstick before vanishing into the bedroom.

"And oddly enough, I got inside without even trying."

"What can I say, David? You won me over with your suave charm and devastating good looks." She said, a faint hint of sarcasm injected in her words. "So, where are we going tonight?"

"Do you like Italian food?"

Her chuckle was barely audible over the violent opening and shutting of drawers in the next room. "As a matter of fact, I love it. I'm part Italian on my mom's side, actually."

"Great. I've got reservations at Olive Garden for 8:45."

She poked her head out from behind the doorway and gave me a look of horror.

"I'm *kidding*," I said, "There's this great little bistro a few miles from here. I think you'll love it."

"Oh, thank god," she said, her beautiful smile returning to her face, "For a second, I thought you were serious."

I was. I laughed and stealthy ducked into the kitchen, quickly pulling my phone out to cancel our reservations. *So she's a bit of a snob. Oh well.*

"Um, yeah, hi. This is David Fox, I have a reservation for two tonight at 8:45?"

I cautiously glanced over divider to make sure she was Nina wasn't listening in.

"Yeah, uh huh. Actually, I was just calling to cancel our reservation... Unfortunately, one of our party members has just become...*ill*. Okay, great, thank you. Have a good one."

I hung up the phone and stepped back into the living room. Much to my surprise, I found Nina standing in the middle of the room, her hands neatly tucked against her hips.

She was wearing a striking red dress that put my pitiful 'collared shirt with khakis' outfit to shame. Her hair, now free of tangles and foreign objects, hung calmly in the air, the long strands of amber perfectly framing her face. Matching her dress, a sort of burgundy, almost bloody red paste was smeared across her lips. Dark eye-liner produced a sort of morbid calmness in her eyes that sent a chill down my spine.

"What were you doing in there?"she asked, interrupting my thoughts.

Shit, had she heard me? Think fast, think fast.

"I...I was just going through your pantry." I replied quickly. Perhaps too quickly. "Checking to seeing what kind of food you usually eat, I wanted to make sure dinner tonight would be fancy enough for you. Judging by the expired milk and half a can of tuna fish in the refrigerator, we should be just fine. Shall we?"

Her stern gaze softened and she chuckled quietly. "You've caught me; I eat out a lot. Let me just get my purse."

Nina leaned over the end table by the couch and stuffed a few possessions into her bag before laboriously hoisting it over her shoulder. I followed her to the door and stepped back out into the hallway. The same sort of sense of danger that I had felt when Tyler and I had broken in here, just a few nights before, filled the air and I glanced nervously up and down the hallway while Nina locked the door. In my mind, I began to fantasize about nosey neighbors who might have inadvertently witnessed the break in entering the hallway and blowing my cover, revealing me for what I was: a fraud.

We took the elevator to the main floor and walked back out onto the landing in front of Nina's apartment.

"Shall I drive, then?" I asked, glancing up the sidewalk to my decrepit pile of nuts and bolts. I caught sight of Nina's car out of the corner of my eye; she drove a badass-looking bright red BMW convertible that on any other day I would have loved to have taken a ride in, but under the circumstances I was very self-conscious of my own pool of knowledge; I shouldn't *know* what kind of car she drove, because as far as she was aware I had never seen her drive it before.

"Sure. I don't know where we're going anyway, and I'm terrible at taking directions."

Oh. *Right.*

I hesitantly thumbed my key into the passenger door of my car and unlocked it. As I tugged on the handle, the warp plastic emitted a deep howl as the bottom of the door scraped against the frame of the car.

"Sorry..." I said, somewhat embarrassed, "My car is pretty crappy." I held the door open as she cautiously climbed onto the seat and then ran around to the driver's side and let myself in.

"I like it," Nina replied, her eyes flitting around the inside of the vehicle, "it's got character. How long have you had it?"

"This was actually the first car I ever bought after I got my license when I was 16," I revealed as I jammed the keys into the ignition and started the car. I prayed the engine was feeling cooperative today and would turn-over after just a few attempts. Much to my surprise, it started on the first go. I guess I was lucky tonight after all. "bought it from a used car salesman named Stan for a thousand bucks. He said it used to be a government vehicle, I think."

"Is that marketing code for 'no drugs covertly stashed in the side panels'?" Nina asked playfully.

I threw the car into reverse and looked over my shoulder, trying to carefully weasel my way out of the parking spot without hitting her car as I responded.

"You know, that never came up on the Carfax report, so I'm not sure..."

Nina laughed at my remark as I pulled out onto the street and started driving towards the next intersection.

"You know, I wish there were those kinds of reports for *relationships*." Anna was thoughtfully staring out her window as we came to a stop at a red light when she next spoke. "It's always good to know what you're getting yourself into when you invest in something..."

Her profound subtext was lost on me at the time, as I was far too busy concentrated on the road and avoiding car accidents, but I was able to form a joke.

"Oh, man, I'm glad there isn't. I'd never get a date again!" I watched Nina raise her eyebrow out of the corner of my eye. "Mine would all be like 'left the toilet seat up 835 nights in a row, has a tendency to walk around house with no pants on, and sings songs from Broadway musicals off-key in the shower' and stuff. It's definitely better to ease the other person into your idiosyncrasies over time. All at once like that is just too much!"

She smirked. "I don't know. I believe in *informed consent*."

"Alright, what should I know about you, then?"

She seemed taken aback for a moment and considered carefully before responding.

"Well, I guess mine would say something like 'has a tendency to go after 'bad boys' and then sabotage the relationship after she realizes they are complete morons who are unable to have a conversation about anything besides sports and the featured article in the latest issue of Playboy'."

"That is...alarmingly specific, Nina." I turned and gave her a wry smile. "If it's any consolation, I'm more of a Hustler kind of guy."

She laughed heartily for a few moments before composing herself. "I'm sorry. I didn't mean to impugn your choice of reading material."

"Don't worry, I'm not upset...but you are going to have to apologize to Mrs. October."

We continue chatting for a few more minutes before arriving at our destination. We drove past the front of the bistro, turning into the side alley to find a parking space.

"Here we are," I said, gesturing to the restaurant's entrance as I shifted the car into park. "Porto Rosalina."

We walked inside the restaurant and I strode confidently up to the young woman behind the podium.

"Good evening. Welcome to Porto Rosalina. How many in your party, sir?"

I held up two fingers and wrapped my arm around Nina's waist. She seemed surprised but didn't offer any resistance. "Just us."

"Very good, sir. This way, please."

The woman grabbed two menus out of a small holster attached to the stand and led us through the bistro. I was surprised at how busy it was. All the other times I had been to Porto Rosalina it had been essentially empty. I wonder why tonight was different?

We were seated at a small table off in a corner, near a large grand piano that sat on a platform which was slightly elevated above the rest of the restaurant. The man playing it was dressed in a tuxedo and wearing bright white gloves. He gave Nina and I warm smile as we passed.

The server offered a menu to each of us and said, "Your waiter this evening will be Tanya. She will be with you in just a moment. Have a pleasant evening."

She smiled and bowed slightly before departing. There was a moment of silence between Nina and myself as we each buried our noses in our menu, deciding on what lavishly produced dish best suited our personal tastes that evening.

Eventually, Tanya waltzed up and started placed glasses of water and small sets of silverware on the table as she greeted us and asked for our drink orders.

"I'll just stick with water, thank you." Nina replied, curtly. She was probably being conservative because she thought the restaurant was above my pay grade. She was right.

"And for you, sir?"

"Let's see... Can we have a bottle of...this Pinot?" I pointed to a line on the wine list. I wasn't sure how to pronounce the name of the vineyard, but it looked expensive-sounding.

"The '03? Certainly, sir. I'll have that for you in just a moment."

Tanya departed and we resumed searching our menus.

"So what are you going to have, David?" Nina asked after a few moments, clearly sensing the mounting anxiety was mutual.

"You know, I really have no idea. I'm afraid to try and order anything off this menu."

She laughed and glanced back at her copy. "I know what you mean. Maybe we *should* have gone to Olive Garden."

I laughed nervously, appreciating the irony. Tanya returned shortly with the bottle of wine and offered it up for me to examine. I nodded, uncertain as to what I really should have been looking for and she set the bottle down on the table and proceeded to uncork it. She poured a thimble-full amount into one of the two wine glasses she had produced and I picked it up.

I strained my brain trying to remember everything I could from a documentary about wine that I had watched a few weeks ago on the food network. It was called 'Wine For The Confused' and talked about all the etiquette about wine that you're supposed to know in order to not make a fool of yourself in situations such as the very one I found myself in that night. Fragments of that esoteric knowledge began to slowly flow through my memory.

I swirled the glass around, careful not to spill any, and held it up to my nose. It smelled...well, it smelled like fermented grapes, I don't know. As long as it didn't smell like wet garbage then you could be pretty sure the wine wasn't 'corked' – which was what you were supposed to be looking for when your waiter offer you the first glass. 'Cork taint' is a phenomenon that occurs due to a fault in the cork manufacturing process which spoils the wine. This often happens either due to a chemical interaction between the wine and bacterial agents on the cork, such pesticidal residue or natural air-bone fungi, or even a structural deformity in the cork itself.

Hoping my intuition was right I set the glass back down on the table and gave the 'ok' signal to Tanya with my hand. She filled my glass and then turned to Nina.

"Madam?"

Nina looked at me for a minute, probably considering if I could afford it, but eventually accepted.

"Yes, please." Tanya placed the second wine glass in front of Nina and began pouring.

"Have you had enough time to decide what you'd like?"

We gave Tanya our respective orders, both clearing trying our best not to embarrass ourselves with our poor pronunciation, and then she departed. I raised my wine glass and smiled at Nina. She followed suit.

"What shall we drink to?" I asked.

She rolled her eyes as if she was trying to recall something.

"To trying something new." I nodded as we each took a sip of our drink.

"Cheers."

One bottle of wine turned into two, which turned into yet another and another. We were at least on our third bottle before our main course even arrived. Nina had ordered some sort of exotic pasta dish with a name I couldn't quite pronounce, and I had settled for a slab of grilled swordfish.

The food was excellent and I had wolfed down my entire meal in no time at all. I spent the rest of the meal, as we talked and the wine continued to flow, watching Nina eat her entrée. I stared intently as she picked at her food, occasionally pushing a pea-sized portion of food onto her fork before reluctantly placing it in her mouth. Every time she managed to do so, she would then quickly hold her free hand in front of her face while she chewed, apparently to spare me the sight of her eating.

It was adorable. I thought to comment on it but having observed the reactions from Anna when her eating habits, quirky or not, were brought to light, I decided that I would refrain. I didn't know Nina well enough to know if she had issues with her body image, and to be honest, I really didn't want to know.

I've always found the relationship between women and their food to be absolutely fascinating. I suppose it is the result of a male-dominated society; we have fortuitously constructed the social contract in such a way that hearty appetites in men are demonstrative of a high survival and reproduction value – 'good genes' – but overindulgence in the fairer sex indicates lack of discipline and 'unattractiveness'.

The night continued on with little incident. We talked and ate and drank and laughed together and I had all but forgotten that our rendezvous was a farce, a scam, a con I was perpetrating on this innocent girl in order to facilitate me winning back the affections of another woman.

After dinner, we headed over to a neighboring cafe to grab a cup of coffee before deciding to a walk though central park, which was a few miles from the restaurant. There was a heavy tension in the air as we slowly strode through the plaza. Nina held her coffee cup close to her chest and played with the edges of her dress nervously.

"So… What kind of music do you like?" I asked, after a few moments, eager to break the awkward silence. "I caught a glance at your collection while we were at your apartment but I never really asked you."

She smiled gently as she replied. "Well, I like to think my tastes are pretty eclectic. I'll listen to anything by any of those sad, whispery indie singer-songwriters that seem to be all the rage now and days. I like a lot of classical stuff too. I like thinks with thoughtful lyrics or things that challenge me to interpret their meaning. I guess that's true of everything I like. Things that aren't exactly what they appear to be at first glance."

I nodded, considering her answer. It made me think about myself. Maybe that was why she was interested in me…she could sense that I was hiding myself from her. That at the end of the day, all of the grandstanding and smooth talking I was able to summon to win her fancy was just a ruse, just a façade that covered up the real, boring, plain old me. But having intuited that, why was she still here…?

"What about you? What kind of stuff are you into?"

"Oh, you know. I love anything with a good beat that you can dance to. I guess it comes from hanging around Tyler so much he always has the craziest soundtracks to his life, since he spends so much time in clubs and parties and stuff. I like electronic stuff too. 8-bit synths always remind me of my childhood."

I smiled as I considered going on a tangent about Tyler and I used to stay up every night after we'd get back from the bar and play online video games until the sun came up, screaming at barely pubescent teenagers every time they killed us, but I wasn't sure I was ready to bare my inner man-child to her, so I quickly moved onto another topic.

"How about movies? What's your favorite film?"

"Hmm…" She put her finger to her lip and let her eyes roll into the back of her head while she tried to decide. "I guess it I had to pick one, it would be *The Notebook*."

"Ha ha, spoken like a true woman!"

"What's wrong with that?" She asked, raising her eyebrow.

"Nothing, I guess. At least you didn't say *Twilight*."

She gave me an evil look and nudged me in the sides with her elbow.

"Hey, I'm sorry!" I said, recoiling from her playfully. "I just hate those kind of sappy romance stories."

"And why is that? Don't you believe in true love?"

"Of course I do, I just don't believe that it comes in the neat little packages that Hollywood and Disney loves to spoon feed to us. Those kinds of things just give people unrealistic ideas of what love and relationships are like, and us regular Joes have to spend our lives trying to live up to the expectation that we should be anything like the perfect people in the stories. But real life isn't like that, there isn't always happy endings that just come to you. Real love is hard, and you have to always keep working at it, but the effort is what makes it worthwhile."

"For someone who claims to 'hate' sappy romance stories, you sure sound like you've seen more than your fair share of them," she replied suspiciously.

"Yeah, well, there was a time when I thought true love worked like that. That just being in love was enough to make all your problems go away."

"But you don't think that way anymore? What happened?"

"I fell in love, with someone who I thought was perfect for me," I smiled sadly as I continued, "but things weren't that easy for us. I thought that if I just loved her enough, everything would fall into place and we could be happy. But in the end, it didn't work out that way..."

I sort of lost track of where I was as thoughts of Anna flooded my mind. Did I really believe what I was saying – that love wasn't enough? That couldn't be right, could it...? It had to be enough, *it had to be...*

Nina cleared her throat, bringing me back to reality. I looked at her and she gave me a kind glance as she took a sip of her coffee.

"What about you, Nina?" I said, unsure if I really wanted to enter the territory my question would take us into. "Have you ever been in *love*?"

She nodded and looked away as she responded.

"Yeah...once. In college."

I could tell I was making her uncomfortable – clearly this wasn't first date material – but before I was able to skillfully change topics, Nina started speaking again.

"My third year at university I started seeing this guy who was in one of my ethics classes, Anthony. He seemed like a really nice guy; nice looking, nice car, nice grades, he was everything I thought I had wanted in a guy. We dated for about a year and we had all these plans about what we were gonna do after we graduated. Anthony wanted to become a Lawyer, so we were going to move to New York where his father's law firm was based out of and start a new life together."

"Sounds fairy tale-esque," I quipped.

"Yeah, it was... it was great. That year was the happiest year of my life, I think."

"So what happened between you guys?"

"Well, the month before Graduation we found out about Rex's condition... We didn't know how serious it was yet, but I was still so scared for him. I was so worried I was going to lose my baby brother that I was too upset to do anything. I stopped going out with my friends, stopped going to parties, and just stayed home all day, trying to figure out how this could happen in my perfect little world where everything was going great. And Anthony... Well... Isn't it funny how the people we need most in times of crisis decide they don't want to be around when you don't shine as brightly as you used to...?"

I frowned and took a deep breath. I knew exactly what she meant.

"I found out the day before graduation that Anthony had cheated on me at some grad party one of his friends had thrown the week before. I wasn't there, because I had flown out to see Rex, since he couldn't make it to the ceremony in his condition..."

Nina sort of trailed off and went silent for a few moments.

"I'm sorry, Nina. That's terrible..." I racked my brain as I tried to think of an appropriate way to change the mood. "Look, let's not talk about our bastard exes okay? It's really bumming me out."

"You're right, I'm sorry." She seemed to regain her usual air of confidence as she spoke, "You never answered your own question, though. What's your favorite film?"

I grinned, happy to see the old Nina back in action.

"That's really tough, but I would have to say *High Fidelity*. Have you seen it?"

"Yeah, I have. I really liked it. It did have a nice fairy tale ending though, so I suppose that's a given..." She winked at me and giggled.

"Yeah, yeah, alright. Let's just change topics. I can tell I'm never gonna hear the end of this one.

She smiled sadly and nodded. "What about art? Are you the museum-going type?"

I shook my head. "Not really... I don't really get most modern art. Like paintings and sculptures and stuff. I don't mind them, and have enough aesthetic sense to be able to feel like a nice painting of a sunset is pleasing to the eye, but I don't know, that kind of stuff isn't very engaging to me. I must have terrible taste, because truth be told I think the Mona Lisa is ugly as hell." I laughed.

"I know what you mean. We used to go to museums all the time when I was a kid. My mother is from old money and she always tried to bring us up with refined tastes for those sorts of things. We went to France one year for Christmas and visited the Louvre, and there was some sort of big opening the day we went so it was really crowded and we had to stand in line for a couple hours before we could get in. Everyone seemed so excited to see everything, but I just didn't get it. It seemed like everyone was just pretending to understand why all these old artifacts were worth standing out in the cold for. Mom loved it, though. So did Rex..."

Her voice trailed off as her brother's name left her lips. She seemed like she was remembering something, so I pressed the topic without really considering the consequences.

"Do you still go to museums a lot?

"I spent last summer traveling abroad and went to lot of exhibitions and things like that around Europe. I hadn't grown to appreciate them much more than I did when I was a kid, but I liked going because they made me feel like I was home. There's something about paintings and sculptures that transcend boundaries like language or time. You don't need to speak French to appreciate Monet, or be religious to see beauty in the painting of the Sistine Chapel. Something's are just timeless. I went to the Louvre and remembered being there with family when I was young and it just felt like no time had passed at all. Rex was supposed to meet me during the trip, but..."

Nina stopped walking and just sort of froze up. I took a few steps more steps forward before realizing she was no longer with me and looked back to her. She was trying to hide her face behind her hair but I could tell she was crying. I took a step forward and held her in my arms.

"Hey, it's okay... Everything's gonna be alright." I cooed calmly, but every word I spoke only seem to intensify her sobs.

We stood there on the path in silence for a moment as she wept into my shirt. Her arms were pressed against my chest and I let my head rest against hers. I had an overwhelming desire to do anything in my power to make her tears go away, but there was nothing I could do or say that would fix what was wrong. Rex was going to die, it was only a matter of time.

I ran my fingers through Nina's hair and stroked the back her head with my fingertips. After a few more moments, her sobs quieted and turned to sniffles. I pulled a handkerchief out of my coat pocket and handed it to her. She smiled and laughed, despite her tears, as I handed it to her.

"*Really*? People still carry handkerchiefs? Thank you..." She rubbed her eyes and blew her nose into it as I responded.

"Hey, everyone's gotta cry sometime." She smiled again and nodded as I fished an errant tear off her cheek with the side of my index finger.

"I'm sorry for breaking down like this, David..." she said, wringing out the handkerchief and handing it back to me.

"Don't be sorry, Nina. Not everyone can deal with all of their problems alone. Sometimes, even the strongest person needs some *help*."

Nina nodded, sighing deeply, and we resumed walking through the park. She shifted the topic of conversation to something else but in the back of my mind I kept thinking about her brother, and how lucky he was to have a sister that loved him as much as Nina did.

We exchanged more banter for a few minutes as I responded to her queries about films and novels. Somewhere along the line, our paths through the park seemed to merge and the distance between us shrank. Her hand found mine and each of our fingertips slid into place between the other's. She would squeeze softly my hand every few minutes, as if to make sure I was still there, and I would squeeze back.

I am here, Nina.

After a time the steady confidence returned to her voice and her eyes no longer looked glassy. I was just about to open my mouth to say something, when suddenly I felt a drop of water splash against the top of my head. And then another, and another one, and then several more in rapid succession. Without any further warning, a torrential down pour of rain began to bombard the park, the gigantic droplets splashing loudly against the pavement as they deployed their payload.

"...Shit," Nina muttered. She certainly wasn't dressed for the occasion.

I grabbed her hand and pulled her off the path, deeper into the park. We raced across the grass until at last we came to stand under a giant old oak tree in the center of the park. It must have been a hundred feet tall and maybe half that around. Its expansive network of branches and leaves offered fairly decent protection against the elements. Nina's breath was short as we sat down on a wooden bench beneath the tree.

"Jesus, David, don't you know anything...? Never make a girl run in heels..."

I laughed as she combed the rain out of her hair with her hand. Standing up, I pulled my arms out of the sleeves of my jacket and wrapped it around the shivering, wet girl.

"I'm sorry Nina, I really had no idea it was going to rain tonight..."

"It's not your fault, David. Actually, I quite like the rain... Well, when it isn't messing up my hair and getting my nicest pair of shoes covered in mud...." she added sarcastically.

"I like the rain too..." I said quietly, not really meaning to share the thought out loud as I stared at her, *"Everything looks so beautiful in the rain."*

Her eyes had begun to wander around the park as I spoke. "Yeah, I—"

She stopped speaking suddenly and her expression softened as her gaze returned to mine. The soft pulse of the rain pouring down all seemed to reflect the trembling of her lips and my heart began to pound in my chest.

I swallowed hard as we looked into each other's eyes, and I knew in that moment what was to come. Nina's head tilted slowly to the side, her eyes sliding closed, and she leaned forward, inviting me to participate in this moment, this feeling that we shared that night, and I reflected her posture, all too eager to accept it.

Slowly, I let my hand drift from my side, extending it towards her as I leaned in. It came to rest on her cheek bone, still slick with tears and rain water. I guided my lips to hers and pressed them into her while my fingers gently held her in place.

I could taste the wine we shared that night, still on her lips, and it was almost as if this were simply one more pleasantry in the night's proceedings, a logical conclusion to a chain of events that was as natural as the parts before it. There was no awkward hesitation as our lips pursed and opened again which each kiss, no reservation in our minds that this was what we wanted most of all, perhaps not a moment ago and perhaps not in the next, but for now, right there under that oak tree in the park, we had exactly what we wanted. *Things were perfect.*

She placed a gentle hand on my neck as the kiss intensified and tongues began to engage in a back and forth, attack and defense, thrust and riposte, as they explored one another's dimensions. Her breath was hot against my face and it warmed me to my soul, chasing the cold away from a part of me that for so long now had beneath an avalanche of sorrow and ice, frozen in time with a girl named Anna, as though it were her play thing, something I had given to her and her alone to admire and appreciate when she chose to and to ignore and let wither away when she didn't.

My mind raced and my heart continued to pound as I moved my hand to the back of her head, gripping her hair tightly to ensure she would not free herself from this embrace without my consent, because although I didn't not know what this experience meant, what half-truths she and I would later tell ourselves to rationalize this capitulation to our hormones, and to convince myself that falling in love with this girl, in this moment, was all 'part of the plan,' I did know that I did not want it to end too quickly, because whatever would come after could not be as good as this, as that *one kiss*.

An eternity seemed to pass as our heavy breathing grew louder and the sloppy suction of our mouths grew damper. I did not know how long it had been by the time we finally relented and pulled back far enough to look into each other's eyes once more.

"Wow…" Nina whispered breathlessly. Her eyes were glassy once more, but her trembling had ceased.

I nodded and planted one last soft kiss on her lips, finding myself completely without words to describe what had just transpired.

"Hey," Nina whispered again, "it stopped raining."

We walked in silence back to the car, her hand once again finding mine somewhere along the path. The periodic squeezing did not return, no longer counting the minutes our fingertips lingered together, until we reached the car and she gave me one final squeeze before withdrawing her hand to open the car door.

"It's getting late," I said, "Do you want me to take you home?"

She nodded and took my hand back, placing it in her lap, and didn't speak a word until we arrived back at her place a few minutes later. I followed her up to the landing by the door, but hesitated on the last step. Anna reached the top of the landing and turned back to face me, she had a smile on her face.

"So, I guess this is where I ask if you want to come up for 'coffee,'" she mused.

Before I could respond, suddenly my phone began to ring. I pulled my phone out of my pocket instinctively, wondering who would be calling this late at night. I should have known. Who else could it be?

"Dude, David, it's me."

"What is it, Tyler?" I glanced up furtively at Nina. "This isn't a good time—"

"Dude, you have to come down here right now. Please, it's an emergency, dude!"

My eyes widened. "What happened? Are you okay?"

"I can't talk about it right now, man. Just please get down here." There was a desperation in his voice that I hadn't heard for as long as I knew him.

"Where are you?"

"I'm on the corner of 4th and Fremont. Please man, I'll owe you big time."

"Okay, alright already. Just hang tight."

I hung up the phone. My heart was racing; what kind of trouble did Tyler get himself into this time? I looked up at Nina, who was staring back at me expectantly.

"So…are you coming up?"

"I... I would love to Nina, *really*, but that was Tyler and I think he's in some kind of trouble or something; he needs me to come help him."

She smirked out of the corner of her mouth and nodded.

"You're a true friend, David. Good night."

"I'm really sorry, Nina. I'll call you tomorrow."

She nodded and opened the door to her complex. She stepped through and offered me one last smile through the plate glass window before disappearing into the elevator. I soaked it in for a moment before hopping into my car and heading toward Fremont.

I read the cross streets as I passed by, and as their numeric values decreased – 8th, 7th, 6th – the environs began to grow more and more dilapidated, the average number of busted out and boarded up windows per building grew ever higher, until at last I arrived on the corner of Fremont and 4th, which was not even a building at all as it turned out, but rather, a parking lot.

I surveyed the scene as I pulled off to the side of the street and parked on the curb. There were dozens, perhaps even hundreds of people scattered across the empty lot, some in tight clusters, others more evenly spaced, and in the middle of it all, the focal point of the orbiting chains of bodies, there was a *fire*. Not just any fire, a spectacularly large flame which flickered and writhed in the evening breeze.

As I stepped out into the street and approached the masses of people, some of whom stared into the inferno vacantly and others more explicitly anxious about the force nervously paced back and forth, I caught site of a familiar form, silhouetted against the orange light.

"Tyler!" I called out, and jogged a brisk pace across the street. He turned awkwardly as I approached, and after a brief look of confusion was followed by recognition, he held out his arms.

"David? Hey buddy! What are you doing here?"

"What am I—Tyler, you called me 15 minutes ago and begged me to come over here. How can you not remember?" Deciding there were more important issues at hand than Tyler's terrible short-term memory, I pressed on. "What happened here?!"

"Did I call you? I don't remember..." He laughed and shrugged before turning back to the towering blaze. "What's happening here is a bonfire, man! Join the party!" He reached into a plastic bucket on the ground and pulled out a beer and thrust it into my hand.

"You...you guys did this?" I said, completely in shock. Tyler's behavior often bordered on criminally negligent, but I had never seen him destroy property before.

"We had to keep warm somehow, that storm came out of fuckin' nowhere, dude!"

I stood there in complete shock for a few moments, struggling find the words.

"So, approximately, how much would you say you've had to drink tonight, Tyler?"

"Honestly, dude," Tyler said as he clumsily cracked open another brew and clinked it against the one I still held in my hand. "I have no fuckin' idea. This party has been going on all goddamn night. I was gonna invite you, but you weren't at your place when I stopped by. Where've you been all night?"

"I was at *dinner* with *Nina*."

"Oh *shiiiiiiit*," Tyler gasped, "How's it going with her, anyway?"

"Really well, actually. We had a really nice time and took a walk in a park after dinner. It was really special."

I sighed deeply, fairly certain that Tyler wouldn't be able to understand the complexity of the emotional intimacy Nina and I had shared that evening when he was sober, to say nothing of arson-level hammered. I decided to speak to him more on his own level of understanding.

"She was actually just about to invite me back up to her place when you called me."

"Oh, fuck, my bad man. I *swear* I don't even remember calling you." He snorted and threw a piece of wood into the fire.

I believed him. It was easy to construct a mental image in my head of Tyler getting so drunk he started a fire, and then getting drunker until he began to panic about it, and then solving that problem with yet more alcohol, forgot about it entirely.

"Oh well, sometimes it's good to build the anticipation a little, right?"

I nodded reluctantly and took a drink of the beer, and stared at all the people in the lot. Any other night I would have launched off the deep end and been chewing out Tyler and everyone else at his little 'shindig'. I would try to control the situation. But for some reason, tonight, I was content to just...go with the flow. The fire crackled and howled in the wind, as if agreeing with sentiments.

"I'm glad you're here though, man. I really am." The drink was clearly speaking for him. "You deserve a have a good time, man. You've been working hard this past month. You deserve some time to relax."

I had no idea what the hell Tyler was talking about, or why he thought bringing me out to watch him commit a felony would make me relax, so I just stood there, in a stunned silence, and continued drinking my beer.

"Sure is a big fire." Tyler said after a moment of silence.

"Yeah. Sure is."

We stood there for a few minutes, Tyler and I, until the soft whispering of the fire and distant laughter of the other people in the lot was eventually overpowered by the echo of sirens.

I questioned the source of the noise for a moment until a bright light, brighter than the biggest bonfire, illuminated the parking lot in its entirety. Tyler and I turned and found two police cars had driven up behind us.

"Good evening, officers!" Tyler called out to them as they stepped onto the pavement. *"Join the party!"*

CHAPTER 15

A frigid numbness washing over my body pulled and tugged at the periphery of my conscious. I was cold...so very cold, but somehow, I felt *safe*. I opened my eyes slowly, the naturally curious segment of my brain overruling the inner sloth-like complacency which was happy to remain docile, comfortable in the arms of this unknown sensation.

A familiar silhouette hovered in front of my face: a lion's head pendant, given to me by my father on his deathbed. My only remaining memory of the man whose love and pride I could not become worthy of before he left this world stayed with me always, reminding me of the cruelty of the human condition: that life is short and tomorrow is never guaranteed.

I reached out to grab it, to hold it close as I often did when answers escaped me. My fingertips grazed against the floating iron for the briefest of moments before the object settled in my palm. Squeezing tightly, I wished away the cold, because I knew this pleasure was like all that came before and all that would come after: fleeting, transitory, deceitful, and I would rather live in enlightened despair than blissful self-deception.

As I pulled my arm to my chest, I noticed something out of the corner of my eye. A transparent pocket of air – a bubble – escaped from a crease in my jacket, and floated away, up into the heavens. I reached out cautiously with a finger, to pop it, when another oddity caught my attention: my finger tips were...pruning. *What was happening to me?*

I let my arms float away from me and leaned back, looking upward. About a foot above my face, a shimmering portal pulsed, bending and obscuring the illuminating light above. My heartbeat began to quicken, and a cyclone of bubbles swirled around my face, a veritable whirlpool of... *That's it.*

I am under water.

Instinctively, I kicked my feet out until they found something solid, and pushed myself to the surface. Coughing and sputtering, I emerged from the murky deep and found myself... in a bathtub?

Not just any bathtub – MY bathtub. I was in my apartment. Why was I taking a bath fully dressed? *Why can't I remember anything?*

I hoisted myself out of the tub, the gallons of water I carried in my clothing encumbering me to the point of paralysis. Something caught my foot as it came over the side of the tub and crashed to the floor with a loud clang, but I didn't care. I landed on the linoleum floor and began to frantically peel back the layers of cotton from my skin – my jacket revealing a sweatshirt, the sweatshirt hiding yet another piece of attire. After what seemed like an eternity of struggling, I was finally free; naked on my bathroom floor.

On the verge of hyperventilating, I looked back, slowly, to the side of the tub. An extension cord was wrapped around the leg of my jeans. Reaching out, I grabbed the cord and unwound it from my pants, and began to follow it, tugging it towards me frantically. Eventually, I found the source of the loud banging noise from earlier. Plugged into the socket at the end of the extension cord was…a toaster? I began to piece together the *what*, gradually, slower than I otherwise might have if my brain was not still water-logged — that the toaster had fallen into the bathtub and electrocuted me — but the *why* still eluded me.

What insanity was this? Why had I desired…on-demand toast while bathing?

I pulled the device free from its power source and set it on the edge of the tub, considering it for a moment. Out of the corner of my eye, I spied my smokes and my lighter, sitting on the lid of the toilet adjacent to the shower. My innate desire for calmness above all else forced my hand to them, and I lit a cigarette and took a drag, the fire inside my lungs warming my entire body which had begun to shake and tremble from the fear and the cold. It was good, incredible, in fact. It felt like I hadn't had a smoke in a thousand lifetimes. Closing my eyes, I searched for answers — I started to ask myself… *'Why?'*

A lit cigarette is poetry in motion. I watch the paper slowly curl and disintegrate, floating away in a wisp of smoke, until the flames begin to burn my fingertips. Where has it gone? What has it become? I cannot help but feel as though I have just witnessed some form of transcendence…and I desire it for myself.

All it takes is the right catalyst. Flesh is like metal; both carry potential in their veins, and when tempered with heat and pressure, the potential surfaces. I want to *burn inside*. I want to become more than what I am. So I take another drag, and feel the fire in my lungs. I hold it in as long as I can, and then exhale slowly, like a death rattle, and watch the smoke escape from my body, every plume taking moments of my life with it. A football game I'll never watch, a dance recital I'll never go to, an anniversary I won't have to remember, all gone. Suicide by inches, I suppose; a slow death, but a sure one, with a measure of control.

I leaned over to ash my cigarette into the marble tray sitting on the toilet, but in my concentrated zen I misjudged the velocity of the ash, and watched it fall over the side of the tray, onto the toilet lid. It began to smoke furiously, and I leaned over to blow it off the porcelain, when I noticed the catalyst: there was a piece of notebook paper on the lid, under the ash tray, now scarred with a black mark of flame. I picked up the tray and placed it next to the toaster, so I could freely examine the sheet.

My eyes flitted back and forth as I skimmed the writing on the page. I recognized my own handwriting, but I could not recall actually writing any of the words printed there. They spoke of sadness and heartbreak and tragedy, and while I was intimately acquainted with these things, I could not imagine when I had chosen now to put those thoughts to page.

Suddenly, my heart began to race again, and I looked around the room frantically. Spotting my cell phone, which had fallen behind the door, I picked it up and hit redial.

Ring. Ring. "David, you know I'm at work. What do you want?" Anna grumbled, clearly not the best of moods. Maybe it wasn't the best time to share my revelations. Unfortunately, my lips moved before my brain could finish processing my options.

"Anna... I think I just tried to kill myself."

"...What?"

I couldn't tell if she was more upset that I had *tried* to take my own life, or disappointed that I hadn't succeeded.

"I...I..." I struggled. What could I say to her that would take back what I've done? *There are no words.*

I swallowed hard. I didn't have enough information to act rationally about this. I had to know why I did what I did. The phone slipped out of my hand and clanged violently against the linoleum floor, the shattering of the plastic case echoing off every wall of the tiny room.

"David?! David, what's happening?!" I could hear Anna shout, but it sounded so very far awake. Like she was falling... "David, I'm coming over!"

"Wait, no, don't—" I yelled back. But it was too late, she had already hung up. The dial tone screeched loudly for a few seconds before finally abating.

Anna worked about twenty minutes away from my apartment. It would take her thirty to get here with traffic. I have half-an-hour to figure out why I did this. Thirty minutes to figure out how to make this okay when she gets here.

My eyes drifted back towards the paper, and I knew I could avoid it no longer. It held the answers I sought.

CHAPTER 16

"What the hell happened...?" I asked Tyler, pulling on the handcuffs that bound us together in an attempt to wake him up. He was out cold but my indignant rage was not going to wait.

"I don't know, man. Things just got out of hand."

"No fucking shit," I replied dryly. "You are un-fucking-believable."

"Oh, this is all my fault, is it?" He replied, indignation spreading through his voice.

"As a matter of fact, it is, yes!" I said, standing up in a futile attempt to move away from him, but our restraints kept us uncomfortably close.

"I'm just trying to help you!" He shot back.

"Help me? Help me?! How does being in jail HELP me?" I cried, my voice rising with each syllable. "How does any of this bullshit you've put me through HELP me, Tyler?!"

I took a deep breath and continued. "I came to you with a *problem*. I've listened to you and followed your perverse orders unquestioningly because I believed you could help me. But you can't even help yourself, can you? How are you gonna talk your way out of this one, Tyler? Gonna seduce a female guard? What does the playbook say about that?"

"A problem. Right," Tyler murmured bitterly, "You know what your problem is? You don't even *know* what your problem is! I *have* been helping you, David. Maybe not in the way you wanted, but I have been getting you through this."

"What the hell are you talking about, Tyler?"

"I never intended to help you get Anna back. I've been helping you get over her." My jaw went slack and I stared daggers at Tyler.

"Have you ever stopped for a second and wondered why you want her back so badly? I know it wasn't because she made you happy, because you've been miserable for as long as I've known you. I know it wasn't for the sex, because you always said she fucked like a fish out of water, so what it is, man? Why is this broad so special? There are plenty of fish in the fucking sea. She's fucking chocolate, man. Find a new fucking bar."

"Enough of your insipid metaphors, Tyler! This isn't about fish! I don't WANT any other fish!"

"Why?! Because you know you might find one that actually makes you happy?!"

"Because Anna is THE ONE! I know that must be hard for you to understand, Tyler, because it's about love and you have no fucking clue in that department, do you? You've never been in love! The only thing you love is yourself!"

"You fucking fraud," Tyler muttered, shaking his head. "You think that for it to be 'true love' it has to last forever. Well, guess what, that kind of shit only happens in shitty teen romance movies and fairy tales. Life's unfair, get fucking used to it! You think tearing yourself to shreds for another five, ten years is going to make her realize what a mistake she's made? She's fucking psycho, man! Even if she did give you another shot, why do you think it would end up any different than all the other times?! Get over it! It's done! There is no 'next time'!"

"Love..." I took a few deep breaths, calming myself, "isn't easy, Tyler. But only cowards give up and run away at the first sign of trouble."

"Cowards live to fight another day," Tyler said, sitting back down. "When was the last time *you* felt alive?"

"The day she left me," I said, taking a seat next to him. "I'm going to get her back, Tyler. I have to. It's the only way."

"You are a stubborn bastard," Tyler said, visibly deflating before putting an arm around me. "but because I love you, I'm going to help you."

I raised my eyebrows and met Tyler's gaze. There was a sad, kindness in his eyes, that I've never seen before.

"You know why I love being your friend?" Tyler started, his eyes starting to mist up. "Because...being around you always makes me feel like I really am that guy I pretend to be. That I can do anything, because you've always believed I could, and I've never wanted to let you down."

"Tyler, I..." I was truly touched. This might be the first genuine sentiment I had ever seen Tyler express.

"And I'm not about to start now. If you believe in me, it's only fair I believe in you. You can get her back, man. I know you will."

"How...?"

Tyler sniffed the tears away and stood up. "I've got a plan. But first, we gotta get out of here."

"And how the hell do you propose we do that?"

He offered a shrug and a platitude to sooth my temper. "Just believe, man. Everything will work out."

"Yeah, well while you're blowing a gasket 'believing', I'm gonna actually do something about it." I walked up to the bars, Tyler in tow, and called out to the guard that was stationed by the door.

"Hey man, don't I get a phone call or something? Come on, where's your Christmas spirit?"

The guard eyed me cautiously for a moment, and after deciding I wasn't a threat handed me a quarter and pointed to a phone at the other end of the holding cell. I pulled Tyler over to it and shoved the dirty coin into the slot. I snatched the phone out of the cradle and held it to my ear. The dial tone rumbled through the receiver.

Who was I going to call? Normally, in a situation like this I would call Tyler, but obviously he was not going be of any help to me now.

I thought of Anna. Maybe, after all that had happened, she would still be willing to help me. It would be an excuse to talk to her again at least... I slowly dialed Anna's number into the phone and held my breath as it began to ring.

Ring. Ring. Ring. She answered on the forth ring, just like she always does.

"Hello?" she said evenly.

I hesitated for a moment, deciding how to respond. A simple 'hi, this is your ex-boyfriend calling from jail' would probably not suffice.

"Hello?!" Anna called, her evident fury growing. I found myself paralyzed, unable to speak lest I incur her wrath, just like I always had. After all these years, nothing had changed. *Nothing ever really changes.*

"I can hear you breathing, you fucking pervert. Who is this?!"

I swallowed hard and hung up the phone. Whatever I thought I might feel after hearing Anna's voice again, it was not what I was currently experiencing. Maybe I never would feel that way again. I turned to Tyler.

"Who did you call?" He asked.

'Nobody', I wanted to tell him. I called nobody important. But I couldn't bring myself to say those words, to say what I knew in my heart wasn't true. Anna wasn't nobody, she was everything to me, she was everything and I couldn't even stand to hear myself say otherwise, even after all this time, I couldn't bring myself to lie to my best friend because of the loyalty I felt for her.

A wave of emotions crashed over my mind and I allowed myself to hate her for a moment, hate that no matter how much she decided she didn't care about me or how quickly she was able to forget about me, hate that every time she had told me she loved me it had been a blatant lie that she had infected my mind with, with the express purpose of hurting me later on, when it suited her. When I had stopped being amusing and she grew tired with the mundane, insipid trials of 'togetherness' she could light the fuse she had carefully stuffed into my heart, from a distance where she would be safe from the shrapnel and laugh her cruel laugh and marvel in the destruction that she had wrought all because of a passing fancy.

I pursed my lips to tell Tyler who exactly I had called, but no sooner had I opened my mouth, than another guard entered the holding area. Shambling up to the bars, he removed a key from the metal key ring attached to his belt and thumbed it into the cast iron lock The cell door slid open with an auspicious rumble.

"Fox, Morris, your bail's been posted. You're free to go."

He reached over and opened the handcuffs that had held us together. I rubbed my wrist for a moment before turning to Tyler in disbelief.

"Who...? One of yours associates, I take it?"

Tyler threw up his arms as I followed him out of the cell. "If you believe, anything is possible."

We followed the guard through the double doors back into the waiting room, where we would meet our mysterious liberator.

"Nina...?!" I practically shouted. She was standing at the main desk, filling out the necessary paper work.

She turned and smiled slightly. "I do hope you boys aren't going to make a habit of this. I can't afford this type of expenditure, even on my salary."

"How did you...know?" She smiled and nodded to Tyler, who shrugged bashfully. "You...called her?"

He leaned in and whispered in my ear, "You don't have to throw back every fish that jumps in your boat of their own free will."

"Thank you kindly for the speedy rescue, Miss Showalter," Tyler continued, "I'd love to stay and chat, but I have a previous engagement which requires my attention."

He turned and called out to the guard manning the checkpoint as he made his way to the desk. "Hey, Steve-o. You got my things? How's your mother?"

"She's doing much better now, Mr. Morris, thank you." The guard replied, retrieving Tyler's personal possessions from the locker behind the desk.

"Give her my best, will ya?" he said, turning back and giving me one last wink before he departed.

"Sure thing, Mr. Morris."

"Ho-ho-ho!" We could hear Tyler shouting as he strolled down the street. "Merry Christmas!" Nina and I looked on in shock for a few moments before turning back to each other.

"I'm so sorry about all of this, Nina. Tyler—"

"is Tyler." She interrupted, "Don't worry about it. This isn't the first time I've bailed a boyfriend out of jail after a night of debauchery and sin."

I smiled at her, considering her words. Boyfriend. *I was her boyfriend?*

"Can I buy you dinner?" I said as we stepped over to Steve's counter to get my effects back. I check my wallet as Steve passed it through the pneumatic divider and made sure there was still money inside.

"Skip the foreplay. Just take me home." She said, throwing her arm around mine as we exited the station and walked down the street, into the night. A frigid blanket of snow fell over us as we moved onward, painting the city with its pure white brushstrokes. The cold nipped at our extremities as we paced slowly down the boulevard, but for some reason, I didn't seem to mind.

Nina and I made love that night, for the first time. It was spectacular. There something primal in the air that night. I'm not going to get into the 'who-did-what-to-who' stuff, but I probably wouldn't be able to piece together a coherent narrative even if I had. It was difficult to perceive anything other than the friction of flesh against flesh soundtracked by a rhythmic symphony of pleasured moans and gasps.

Lying there in-between rounds of passion, sweaty and glistening, I broke the silence.

"What're you doing Saturday night?"

She laughed. "Already thinking ahead, are we? You don't have to be so insecure, I'm not going anywhere. I'm not done with you...yet." She smiled evilly and ran her soft fingers along my chest.

"No, no, it's not that, it's just...there's this New Year's party Tyler's hosting, over at some mansion in the hills. He does it every year, maybe you've heard of it; they call it the 'ho-ho-hoedown'. It's kind of a big deal, everyone dresses up real nice and shit. I was wondering if you wanted to go."

"Yeah, he invited me. I was already thinking of asking someone to go with me," she replied, nonchalantly, running a hand through her hair.

"What?!" I practically shouted, "Who?"

She smiled and climbed on top of me, kissing my neck. "You."

CHAPTER 17

I dressed myself slowly, in an attempt to avoid the task at hand. I told myself that it was so Anna wouldn't find me in such a undignified state, but it wasn't like she hadn't seen me naked before. What was the point?

Eventually, I had nothing else to distract myself with and returned to the bathroom. I pushed aside the damp pieces of clothing which had begun to leak water all over the floor and took the scrap of paper in my hand. Despite my apprehension, I began to read:

To Whom It May Concern:

Tonight, August 16th, I, David Fox, have decided to take my own life. I wanted to leave a note, something that would explain the reasoning behind this selfish act, something that would vindicate my friends and loved ones of responsibility, but as I write these words I find I can muster no empathy for any of them. I am too consumed by my own fears and regrets to think of anyone but myself, and this knowledge – that I have become that which I always knew in my heart was so, a true, dyed-in-the-wool psychopath – leaves me no alternative but the endeavor I have put before me.

I have no wealth, no possessions to divide amongst my kin in this last will and testament, and so I must offer the one thing I do possess and may freely mete out at my discretion: truth. To list the lies I have told and deceits I have perpetrated on innocent people throughout the duration of my life would take months, years – time that I no longer have – but this does not trouble me. There is only one person that truly deserves honesty from me, and it is to this person I wish to address the remainder of this letter.

If you are in receipt of this note, please read no further, and ensure that it finds its way to Annabelle Marie Roberts. This is a dying man's last request, and I trust that your conscience weighs on you as heavily as mine does on me, and forces you to fulfill this task.

I swallowed hard, and turned the page, revealing another sheet of paper, filled with even more madness than the first.

Anna:

Before I begin, I must say this: what has happened is not your fault. I did this to myself, because I am a coward. I hate that I bring this upon you, but I know it is the only way either of us will find peace. We are soul mates, Anna, destined to collide with one another for as long as we live. I cannot live with that knowledge on my soul on longer.

You told me once that all you wanted from me was honesty. In reflection, I'm sure this will seem too little, too late, but you deserve to know the things that drive me. You deserve to know who I am.

Do I regret us? Yes and no.

I love you so much and every second that we are apart is a second that I am not complete. But every second that we are together is a second that you are settling for less. I am so sorry that I pulled you back into my little world. It was selfish and cruel. No one should ever have to live here.

When you first agreed to take me back, I was so excited and happy, but the minute you stepped out the door I felt sick to my stomach. I realized what I had done. Do you know what is like to live knowing every day that it's only a matter of time before you hurt the person you love? Worried that every word you speak might be the one that breaks their heart?

I always thought it was stupid to think that people can meet their soul mates in high school; that that sort of sappy romantic thinking was unrealistic and self-defeating. But I carried on, spending every night for the past five years of my life lamenting over you; my high school squeeze that I just can't get over. I've made you the answer to all my problems over the years, and I feel guilty about that, because there's so much riding on this. If this didn't work out, I knew I wouldn't want to live anymore. It's just too hard to find out the thing you've been wanting for so long doesn't want you too.

I hate it when you ask me what I'm thinking. Not because I don't want to tell you, but because I can't. Because I'm so afraid. Because I don't want to hurt you.

I've wanted to die for so long, but it wasn't an option. I knew it would make you sad again.

I liked it better when I coveted you from afar. It was safe. I couldn't hurt you with my eyes, my thoughts, the letters I would write but never dare send. The nights I would sit outside your apartment and imagine knocking on the door or throwing pebbles at your window. But even in my fantasies, another man would answer the door. There would be two silhouettes in the window frame. I'd walk home in the rain and come to a bridge, at night, when it was as dark as it gets. Staring down into the river, I'd find myself. And you never would.

Search as you might, you'd never know what happened to me. Maybe I moved to France. Maybe I changed my name. And soon, the memories would get fuzzy. Eventually, you wouldn't even be able to remember my name. And then I'd be gone, like a dream you can't quite remember. A me-shaped hole in your heart that you can fill with something else, like a hobby or a past time, or maybe someone new. Someone who would know what to say when you were upset, someone who would remember your anniversary and your mother's birthday, someone who would get you white roses just because its Wednesday. Because white was always your favorite color.

I'm just a hypocrite. How can I claim to love you while knowing I'm preventing you from being with him?

Every time we fight about little things like me leaving the toilet seat up or me thinking your roommate is cute, I panic. I know our relationship isn't strong enough to withstand these repeated stresses. I'm not strong enough either. The only thing keeping us here is nostalgia, and once the pleasant sepi- toned memories recede, you will be gone again.

I remember the first fight we had. I drove home drunk and you were furious with me. It was stupid, I know, but I couldn't understand why you were so angry. But now I do. I put us BOTH in harm's way. For better or for worse, I'm a part of you now.

I grabbed a scrap of paper from the trash that night, while you were in the bathroom, and I wrote you a letter. I tried to break up with you, because I knew that would be for the best. It's only a matter of time until one of us can't stand it anymore. Until one of us crashes our car on the highway. Until one of us dies, and leaves the other all alone. It's better if we get it over with now, before it's too late. Before we get married or have kids or move into together. Before we get trapped.

In the end, I couldn't give you the letter, because I am too selfish to make that kind of sacrifice.

Do you remember that night you did acid with your roommate and asked me to babysit you guys? I keep going back into it in my mind, over and over again. Turning it around and examining its dimensions, hoping to make sense of it. But every time I learn something new, I forget something I had already learned.

I got in my car and drove over, but you both were already freaking out by the time I got there. You just had to watch The Wall immediately, but you didn't have it, and I didn't have it, so you did what you do best; call up your stable of male suitors and see if you can extort what you want from them with promises of attention and friendship.

As I listened to the short, extremely unfriendly conversations with every guy in your address book, I began to realize: that's what our conversations are like. You want something from me, I can't provide it, so you get mad. A slight variation in the Earth's rotation and perhaps it would have been another male acquaintance here, watching over you, while I was called in search of the movie.

The difference with me is, when you do that to me it fucks me up. It seemed like most of the people you called had gotten used to these sorts of short, emotionless exchanges. I still haven't. Every time you talk to me that way, I feel like I have failed. What have I done to incur her wrath? Why can't I act more like she wants me to?

Lying down in the golf course, you told me you heard that one of my ex-girlfriends had recently become a stripper. Oh, Rachel... I'm so sorry.

Here I am, feeling sorry for myself lately because I don't have a good grasp on life, but I look around me and what do I see? Everyone I know is either a burnt-out druggie or a stripper. I'm so glad I didn't let that happen to me. I thought my fear of drugs was pretty neurotic, but I can see firsthand the effect it has on people's lives. They just become...without purpose.

Rachel especially was hard to take. I really liked her. Honestly, and truly I can say without reservation I loved every single thing about her. She was cute, she had the brightest disposition, and yet she was always able to speak with profundity about whatever intimate subject was breeched. She had so much potential. She was a gifted thespian and an esteemed member of the debate club. She had her demons, of course, but don't we all?

And now look at her. Taking her clothes off for money.

It's so hard for me. I seek out broken women because I have dreams of helping them. I want to be someone's shining knight. And then when they push me away and their lives inevitably crumble, all I can do is quietly whisper, "I could have saved you..."

But I can't. You can't save people from themselves. But that doesn't stop me from wanting to try...I feel in earnest I could have helped her make something of herself. I could have provided the anchor she needed.

I feel like I should find out where she works and go there. And watch her. And see if she even recognizes me. Maybe the sight of a friendly face would be enough to shock her out of it. It's never too late...

You went out again last night, to see him. I'm not mad, really. It's understandable. You have a grumpy, socially-retarded boyfriend. Who could blame you wanting a night of normalcy with another human being you can actually relate to?

I know that's not why you're doing it, though. You don't want him. You're just being polite. He's only in town one night, he says. You asked my permission, which I thought was funny... Who I am to tell you not to do anything? How could I stop you? Even if I were the jealous type, I'm not controlling enough to try to stop you from seeing him, or self-confident enough to think your desire to see him was wrought out of anything other than my own inadequacies.

Do I want you to stop seeing him? Yes, but I wouldn't tell you that. What I want more is for YOU to want to stop seeing him. I want you to never want to look at another man again. I want you to think all other men to be nothing but a cheap knock off of me. I want to be the center of your world.

But I know that's unreasonable, and probably unhealthy, so I'll keep quiet. I'll just hope you come to that conclusion on your own. If I was a better man, you just might.

It's not a matter of trust; I know you're not cruel enough to wound me in the way which would hurt me the most, but at the same time...I know you're what you're capable of. You've done it before. You've cheated. You cheated on him...with me.

It's funny, as I turn the page to continue, it occurs to me that this is the longest piece of prose I have ever written. I call myself a writer, even though

I've never actually written anything. I've tried, time and time again, to put pen to paper, and write what I feel.

But I don't understand what I feel. I feel so many things all at once, there's no possible way that I can isolate one stand of consciousness long enough to describe it before it morphs and changes into the next hideous specter and submerges back into the murk of my mind.

Hideous, black things pull at my heart and every night I fight back, and try to reclaim some of the space so I can fill it with thoughts of you. The darkness retreats for a time, and I tell myself that it's all better. That I won't have to live like this anymore.

Then I let my guard down, and it creeps back in, until it's on the edge of me, looking down into the abyss. It shrieks and howls as it pumps through my veins and it tears its way back into my heart. I can't stop it. It's a part of me now.

Late at night, when I'm driving to your place, I go down the steep hill by the highway, into the valley. It's so dark up there, and the car goes so fast. Every time I'm out there, I worry that in the dead of night, the darkness inside me is going to take over. I won't speed up suddenly or jerk the wheel across the road, I'll just...let go.

Then, I think about our children. The one's we didn't have yet.. God...they were going to be so beautiful. Aiden, and Natalie. A boy and a girl, just like we wanted. They were going to grow up to do amazing things... And now, they're gone.

I'm worried that I will poison your mind the way they poisoned me. I'm worried this sickness is contagious. What if our children have to bear this burden? What if they go through life not understanding why they are the way they are?

I can't let that happen. I inherited this too.

Then, I think about sex. I hate sex. I dream of being some sort of amazing sex god who can bring any woman to ecstasy, but no matter how many books I read, or how many women I am with, I cannot make any of them come. They all tell me that it's okay, that it doesn't happen for them every time, that I am still the best they have ever had. Some of them may be telling the truth, many are probably just being charitable, but in either case it is a poor consolation prize. Who can spend the rest of their lives with someone who does not sexually satisfy them?

Their pain is my own. They may fake orgasms, but I fake everything. The moans, the gasps, the desperate proclamations of love and ecstasy. I feel nothing. I fake interest in the act, but I am somewhere else. I am taking the SATs, or playing the grand piano in front of my third grade teacher. I am performing for an audience of one, and it's never quite good enough. There's a cold, calculated, methodical pattern to my technique that I cannot escape. Sexual mastery requires a certain amount of spontaneity, but I feel like I am just solving a math problem. There are X amount of positions. There are Y amount of ways to touch her. There are Z amount of sexual configurations. How long before we have run out? My normal approach is useless here.

As you dig your nails into my back, I am watching hands on the clock. How long have we been doing this? Should I go faster? Are you really enjoying this or just pretending? What will you tell you friends? Why won't you look at me?

It's too impolite, I guess. To come before you do. So I wait, and wait, and I wait. I hear the same pattern of moans escape your lips, over and over again. I fantasize about covering you in my love juices, like a dog marking its territory. But when the time comes, I can never do it. I can't degrade you like that. This has to mean something more.

You think it's cute to tease me. To be coy and play shy. You love seeing me beg for it. But I hate it. I hate that you don't want me as much as I want you. So I take you by force, and pretend you're just playing hard to get, that somewhere in inside you there is an atom of your being that burns with passion for me. That maybe you think the same disgusting, filthy thoughts about me that I think about you.

Eventually, hours later, I give up. I can continue the charade no longer. If it was going to happen, it would have happened by now. One last faked grunt and a shudder, then I collapse. There's always next time.

Sex is a part of a healthy relationship, right? So why is it so hard for me? Why do I always end up feeling like the bad guy every time I breach the topic? Why do I get the feeling that if it were up to you we'd never have sex again?

I asked you once; if you were sure you loved me. You took it the wrong way; I was never concerned about your authenticity or sincerity. I knew your affection for me was as genuine as it could be; 5 years later, you still wanted to put up with my bullshit. You were nostalgic for the endless nights and countless fights we shared. I missed them too, in a way.

But what I meant was that are you sure you loved ME? The real me, not the people I pretend to be every day. I wear so many masks, I wouldn't blame you if you fell for one of them instead. Maybe I wouldn't even care. Loving a persona I had created is almost as good as the real thing, and if we both kept the act up long enough, maybe it would come true. I can't help but feel like there's a side of me you've never seen. And if I have my way, you never will.

Who am I? Really? I'm not sure I even know that anymore. When you wear so many masks for so long you begin to forget what you were underneath. And if you try to take off those masks, you risk pulling off the skin right along with it.

There have been so many of 'me' over the years. The cruel child, the arrogant intellectual, the morose loner — maybe they're all pieces of a greater whole. But I will tell you this: I never liked any of them. That's why I kept changing.

It started in high school, I guess. I show up, in this new place, filled with cruel school children, bound by a myriad of unspoken, unfair rules I could never understand. No one knew me, no one wanted to know me, and all I wanted to know was why.

I couldn't accept the fact that I had no friends; even as self-effacing as I am I knew that I surely had at least some qualities that at least one out of the two-thousand people I passed by on a daily basis would find appealing, or at least promising enough to give me a chance. But no one did. No one liked the things I liked or thought the things that I thought or felt the way that I felt. I had to change. So I did.

But I messed up. I didn't conform, but not because I had a 'mind of my own', I just didn't know how. I didn't know how to watch MTV or like rap music or buy expensive clothing or use cool slang. These concepts were foreign to me. So I gave them reason to hate me. I became that asshole that you know and love. If they hated me, I'd hate them back twice over, and then blame it on misunderstanding. They didn't hate ME really; they hated 'him,' the guy I pretended to be. If they just got to KNOW me, really, I'm sure we'd get along great.

Or at least that's what I'd tell myself.

I'd sit in the park at lunch time and watch the cars pass by. Poisonous envy would drip in my heart and tell me 'you can be like them, if you just TRIED,' but I was too scared. Scared of becoming another teenage cliché. I didn't see excitement and experimentation in the high school experience. I saw darkness. I was afraid of the sex and the drugs and the booze and the lies and the murder. That would be the end of me.

I took refuge in my ivory tower. I told myself I was better than them, and that I would never sink down to their level. But it sure was lonely up there. Maybe crossing over WOULD have killed me, but at least then I wouldn't have had to die alone.

I've often thought about how I would die. Whether or not it would be in an accident, or by natural causes, or if eventually, I just decided it wasn't worth it anymore, and, well...you know.

I read a news article once about a family who tried to kill themselves by turning the gas in their apartment and waiting. The gas seeped down through the floor and killed their downstairs neighbors instead. You have to research these things.

I found a website on the internet once, when I was a kid. It had a list of hundreds of possible ways to take your own life, and rated them based on painfulness, efficiency, and gore. I went through each entry and fantasized each possible configuration, but I couldn't make up my mind. I went back and forth between gun to the head and taking a bottle of Tylenol with gin. All of the good ones seemed impossible to pull off. Where would I get the cyanide capsules? Could I really drink 14 liters of water without passing out first?

It would have to be something quick. If after I had initiated the act, I had time to contemplate things, I'm sure I would go to every length to undo what I had done. That's human nature, right? To stay alive. I couldn't give my reptile brain a chance to react. I'd have to trick it.

I didn't want it to be messy either. No landlords or girlfriends or elderly neighbors looking to borrow some sugar and stumbling upon my fetid, rotting remains. Chunks of brain matter sliding down the wall. That's just too cruel. I'd write a note first, and stick it on the door. Make things easy for everyone. Just because someone has died doesn't mean we can't be civil about things.

I'd be real orderly about it. Make sure my affairs are in order before I go. The last thing I want are my relatives arguing about what should go on my gravestone. I'd have to write a suicide note, too. You know, let my parents know it wasn't their fault, that sort of thing. I'll tell them I loved them (lie) and that they shouldn't feel bad (lie) and that they did everything they could to help me (lie). I'll tell you that you can get remarried, that it won't dishonor my memory. I'll staple the note to my will and my ATM card and a piece of paper with the password to a computer full of child pornography. That way they can think of me as a villain. They don't have to mourn my passing, I was just a pedophile.

But maybe it would be better if I made it look like a blameless accident. You know, maybe I was just so tired coming home from work, I fell asleep in the garage, in the car, with the engine still on. I went quietly in my sleep. If I could get my hands on some potassium chloride, I could give myself a heart attack.

The coroner might not be able to tell it was suicide. My family lives the rest of their lives thinking there was nothing they could have done, that there was no way to have seen this coming. That I was happy and lived a fulfilling life which was tragically cut short by a cruel and merciless god.

No, I want them to hate me. I want them to look upon my lifeless body and say, 'You coward. You did this to all of us. We're all in that coffin with you.' I want to be burned in effigy. Hate me, Anna. If you want to honor my memory, then do everything you can to hate me. It's the only way.

Goodbye. I love you so much.

-David

The ink of the last sentence started to bleed, moistened by the tears which had streamed down my face and plummeted onto the paper as I held it tightly. But despite the tears, which seemed like they would never cease to flow, I... I was smiling. It took a five years and a near-death experience, but I was finally able to face myself. Everything I had written down on these pages, nearly a manuscript in its length, was as true as I knew how to be.

I swallowed hard and stood up, holding the paper in front of me. No matter how much I wanted her to truly know me, no matter how much I desired for her to read these words on this page, I knew giving this to her, now of all times, would be a selfish act. As selfish as the note itself.

This wasn't for her. It was for me.

There is no amount of objective truth that could be worth the pain and sadness the words I had written would bring her if her eyes fell upon my work. I wasn't really being noble by sharing these dark thoughts, was I? I was trying to hurt her, so that she would know how much she had hurt me. This was cruelty beyond reproach.

My internal dialogue was interrupted by a frenzied knocking at the door.

"David?!" Anna called out through the entryway. "David, it's me!"

I froze in my tracks. I had to get rid of this. I couldn't hide what I had done, it was too late for that, but I could at least spare her the greatest sadness of all.

"David! Open the door!" She called again. I could hear her fiddling with her keychain. I had given her keys the place a few months ago, but she never had reason to use them until now.

I sprung into action. I pulled the lighter out of my pocket, and rolled my thumb across the flint. It took several tries due to the shaking in my hand but eventually I was able to produce a flame. I held it to a corner of the stack of paper and watched the fire begin to eat my words, and spirit them away into the heavens. It spread slowly at first, gaining momentum with each letter it consumed, until at last, it was extinguished. Anna pushed her keys into the lock and practically kicked the door open, but it was too late, the fire had done its job.

I threw the tiny burnt scraps of letterhead into the bath, and stepped out into the living room, catching Anna's gaze as she threw her bags onto the floor. She looked at me with shock, horror, sorrow, and anger, all at the same time. You've really never experienced the full nuance of human emotion until you've told your girlfriend you tried to kill yourself.

"I'm sorry." It was all I knew how to say to her. Now, and forever, I would be just that: sorry.

"I'm sorry, Anna." I repeated it again as she began to slowly move across the carpet towards me. "I'm so sorry."

Just as I finished the third reiteration of my plight, a burst of air whooshed by my face. My neck jerked to the side, and suddenly my cheek felt raw. I looked to Anna, uncertain of what I had just experienced, and her eyes, full of angry tears, told me everything.

She slapped me.

I stood there for a moment, unsure how to proceed. I deserved it, certainly, but I wasn't sure of the protocol for behaving around suicide survivors. She took another step towards me and threw her arms around me, sobbing violently into my shirt. I let my own arms fall upon her back, and I held her close to me. What a fool I had been, to try and throw this all away.

"I'm sorry, Anna. I'm sorry."

CHAPTER 18

Tyler had arranged for a limo to pick me up at my apartment the night of the hoedown. I had dressed myself in the only suit I owned, the pinstripe one I wore to everything: job interviews, weddings, funerals, you name it. This suit had been through the wars with me, but I like it. I looked good in it. Damn good.

I had expected the limo to contain gaggles of Tyler's friends and acquaintances, but as the driver opened the door for me, and I stepped in, I found that it was empty. I tried to give him directions to Nina's place, but he told me "Everything has been taken care of, Sir."

I didn't know what he meant at the time, but I would later come to realize that Tyler was a better friend than I could have ever imagined.

20 minutes later we pulled up in front of Nina's apartment building, and she buzzed me up. I knocked cautiously on her door a few times, and then it opened, revealing the most gorgeous woman I had ever seen in my life.

I stepped in, eyes wide and mouth agape, completely at a loss for words.

"Nina, I... You... wow."

She was wearing this absolutely stunning little black dress, matching stiletto high heels that made her almost as tall as me, and her hair was held up with an elaborate series of clips and ribbons that I couldn't make heads or tails of.

"Well? How do I look?"

"You look...incredible."

"You're not so bad, yourself, handsome." She said, yanking my tie back into place and dusting some lint off my jacket. She grabbed her purse off the sofa, and locked her arm with mine. "Shall we?"

I helped her into the limo, and she began to speak.

"Wow. Tyler's really outdone himself, this time. An entire limo? To ourselves?"

I shrugged, and removed a bottle and glasses from a side compartment in the door. "Tyler takes care of his friends. Champagne?"

We sat and drank and talked for what seemed like an eternity before at long last the limousine came to a halt. I peered through the tinted windows at the house. It was amazing, like a castle almost.

"Wow..." Nina cooed as she stepped out onto the walkway. "This place is amazing. Whose house is this?"

"I don't know, Tyler's probably."

She turned back to me and raised an eyebrow. "What does he do again?"

"Tyler? He does whatever he damn well pleases." I handed the limo driver a crisp twenty dollar bill and strode up to Nina's side, offering my arm. "Shall we?"

She smiled and looked down her nose at me. Biting her bottom lip, she took my arm.

"Let's," she replied, her faux-haughty tone mirroring my own.

We walked up the brick pathway to the front door. At the top of the landing, the mahogany double doors ushered us into the gothic mansion with a somber grace. We entered the foyer, walking briskly to escape the chill. A tall, well-dressed man stood behind a desk by the entrance, fondling a clipboard. He smiled and bowed as we approached.

"Good evening, sir. Good evening, madam. May I have your names please?"

"David Fox and Nina Showalter," I offered, curtly. These sorts of formalities were beneath Tyler. The idea that he would exclude anyone from a party just because their names weren't on a list was absurd. Why was he doing this? It hadn't been like this last year, had it?

The man scanned the list for a few moments, as Nina and I exchanged uncertain glances. What horrors had Tyler constructed tonight? What games were we about to be subjected to as a part of his 'plan'? I shouldn't have let it go this far...I shouldn't have trusted his stupid plans. This was a mistake.

Cold sweat began to form at the sides of my face as the man finished marking our names off the list with an expensive looking pen.

"This way, please."

We followed him towards the doors on the other side of the room. He placed his hand on the door handle, and began to swing the door open for us.

"Enjoy your evening."

As the door swung on its hinges, a hot wave of sound and energy flew over us. Rumbling bass from the stereo system shook the narrow corridor, punctuated by the rhythmic chatter of people being social. We stepped forward through the doors, into the ball room, and our eyes grew wide with shock.

"Wow." Nina gasped. I nodded, unable to think of anything to add to her sentiment.

It was amazing. Golden streamers hung from the vast array of chandeliers dangling from the ceiling. A thin mist poured out of smoke machines tucked into corners behind speakers and tables, bending the flickering light of the disco balls that pulsed and scattered with every scratch of the record. And the people...there were so many people. Hundreds, maybe even thousands of sharply dressed men and women crowded the dance floor from the doorway where we stood, to the far side where the walls opened up into the equally crowded balcony. Screams and hollers of jovial people, laughing and drinking and dancing. There was electricity in the air, a palpable current, a buzz that seemed to entrance every person in attendance. Tyler had given this night to them, and they would be forever grateful.

"After you," I said, motioning to a break in the crowd that would allow us passage.

Nina smiled and led the way through the throngs of people until we found ourselves in the center of the party, the heart of the night's festivities, the lifeline. We talked amongst ourselves for a few moments, marveling at the splendor before us, still calibrating our internal states to the overpowering energy that flowed through the house. I grabbed Nina's hand, and was about to lean in to say something to her, when a familiar voice penetrated the crowd and sent a chill down my spine.

"David?"

I turned, slowly, not sure if I had really heard what I thought I had heard. I closed my eyes, praying that when I opened them my fears would be allayed and the apparition that haunted me would not have materialized. I wasn't ready yet! I needed more time, I—

"David, it *is* you." I exhaled deeply and opened my eyes, watching her approach in slow motion.

"Anna."

"It's great to see you, David. How are you?" There was a sarcastic undertone to her voice. Yeah, I bet it was great to see me. Great to know that I was still circling the drain, great to see that I was still around, waiting to be walked all over again the moment it suited her.

"What do you care?" I replied darkly. I wasn't ready for this. I needed to talk to Tyler. This wasn't part of the plan...

"David, I..." Anna seemed taken aback, unsure what to say. I took the moment to compose myself and noticed the man hovering around her. He looked familiar to me... It couldn't be...could it?

"Nick."

Nick cleaned up well; I had to admit, he was almost unrecognizable without the trademark five o'clock shadow and hoodie that smelled like weed. I extended my hand and smiled wryly. He took it, somewhat begrudgingly.

"Dave."

Funny, I didn't remember him having a lisp before. He hadn't, had he? I'd remember something about him that was that ridiculous, surely. My eyes wandered to a slight swelling on his lip, and suddenly everything became clear. I leapt on it like a hyena devouring a rotting carcass festering in the midday sun.

"How's the jaw?" I drew out my words, emphasizing each syllable clearly.

"Better. *Thanks*." He withdrew his hand and placed it in his pocket, giving me the dirtiest look I had ever seen one man give to another. I could tell it was taking all his willpower not to tackle me to the ground right then and there. Anna must have prepped him, warned him not to make a scene. *The coward.*

Nina cleared her throat and stepped out from behind me. "Sorry to interrupt the pissing match, but aren't you going to introduce me to your friends?"

"Ah, erm, yes, Anna, Nick this is…"

"Nina Showalter," Nina stated confidently as she pushed past me to shake their hands, "a pleasure to meet you."

Nick grunted and nodded at her, while Anna made more pointed attempts at civility.

"Nina, that's a beautiful name. My grandmother's name is Nina. She's so *wise*."

I knew damn well that Anna didn't have a grandmother named Nina. I also knew that 'wise' was a female code word for 'old'. Who was having a pissing match now? Nina smiled politely and nodded, an uncomfortable tension filling the air.

"Well, it was good to see you guys. We were just going to get a drink, excuse us." I pulled Nina's hand through the crowd over to the bar.

"Gin and tonic, please," I growled throatily at the bartender, "more gin, less tonic."

He pushed the drink across the bar and I scooped it up, pouring it down my throat in one deft motion.

"Who *were* those people?" Nina asked suspiciously, "Did you get into a fight with that guy?"

I used my tie to wipe the rogue tonic from the corners of my mouth and confessed. "Yeah. Well, it wasn't so much a 'fight' as a 'I punched him in the face while he was sleeping and then ran away'."

Nina laughed. "Sounds very honorable! Why did you do it?"

I shrugged and ordered another drink. "Fucker deserved it, he…"

I paused to consider. He what? He *stole* from me? Did I really believe that? Nick hadn't taken anything from Anna she hadn't willingly relinquished to him. He did nothing wrong, yet he was the one I struck in anger. What kind of sense did that make?

"He what?" Nina pressed.

I began to cobble together another lie in the back of my mind, but before anything concrete could materialize another voice called out from behind me.

"There he is! My man, glad you could make it!" Tyler. Peering out at us through dark glasses and a pimp hat, Tyler welcomed us to his gala affair.

"Tyler," I started, throwing my arms around him. "This is amazing. Completely over the top, but I've known you far too long to expect anything less."

"What can I say? I do what I do when I do what I do." Tyler babbled profoundly. "Nina. Damn girl," he cooed, taking Nina's hand and planting a delicate kiss on the back of her palm. "If I wasn't afraid Dave would go apeshit on my ass, I'd have half a mind to chase you up and down this dance floor. You looking *good* tonight."

"Erm, yes," Nina replied hesitantly, freeing herself from Tyler's grasp. "It's just as well you don't, I've just had a first-hand look at the devastation David leaves in his path when he feels another man has wronged him. A black eye wouldn't suit you at all."

"I'm a lover, not a fighter, baby." Tyler laughed, tipping his hat. "Speaking of which, do you mind if I steal your boy toy for a minute? I've gotta have a heart to heart with my bro and I don't want any women around getting the notion that I'm some kind of sensitive sap."

"Of course. I think I'll find the ladies room and freshen up a bit. All the alpha male pheromones are making me a bit weak in the knees. Excuse me."

"Nina, wait, I—"

"Don't worry about me," she said giving me a peck on the cheek, "Girls know how to have fun too."

We watched for a moment as she returned to the dance floor and started getting her freak on. Our heads cocked to side in erotic fascination.

"Damn." Tyler said, "I'm beginning to think I made a huge mistake."

"It's too late to back out now," I reminded him. "We've come this far."

"Right you are," he said, putting an arm around my shoulder and leading me through the house. "The flower has just about blossomed." He suddenly took on a hushed tone, pulling two glasses of champagne off a waiter's tray as they passed by." You seen Anna yet?"

I took a sip of the champagne and nodded. "Yeah, I...I didn't handle myself very well. She just sort of snuck up on me, I wasn't expecting it. I might have fucked this whole thing up."

Tyler raised his eyebrows and pointed past me, out to one of the side balconies. "I'm not so sure about that."

I followed his gaze and looked through the glass panes behind us. They perfectly framed the scene; Anna and Nick stood out on the terrace, each gesturing wildly and pacing back and forth in turn.

They were having a fight.

"To be honest, I don't think it mattered what you said. Nina did all the hard work."

"What do you mean?" I said, watching Nick storm off, back into the house, before I turned back to Tyler.

"Well, here you are, looking handsome and dapper with a beautiful woman in your arm, and there she is, stuck with her burnt-out loser boyfriend with a speech impediment."

I chuckled and grinned madly. "You noticed it too?"

He smirked and cocked his head. "He's been telling people he got a tongue piercing, but I happen to know for a fact the only metal in mouth is the wiring holding the hairline fracture in his jaw together."

We burst into laughter together for a minute before resuming our serious tone.

"Okay. What do I do?"

Tyler shook his head grimly. "I can't help you anymore," he said. "I've taught you everything I know about making women want you. What you do with that information is in your hands now. The only question that remains is, will you use that knowledge for good...or evil." He paused between words and pulled his glasses down his nose, looking furtively between Nina, on the dance floor, and Anna, out on the balcony.

"Wait, what? But I—"

"It's up to you now, Dave." He patted my shoulder and began to walk off. "Follow your heart. I know you'll figure it out. Make me proud, kid."

I stood breathless and watched Tyler disappear back into the crowd. A sense of helplessness and anger washed over me. Why had he done this? Why had he abandoned me when I needed him most? Was this all just a game to him, building me up to watch me break down?

I pulled on my tie, loosening its vice like grip around my neck, and steeled myself. I didn't need him. I could do this. All his games and cheap parlor tricks had served me well until now, but we had hurtled past that point. No clever turn of phrase or canned one-liner was going to help me now. I knew something that Tyler didn't. I knew about love, and that would see me through the trial ahead.

    I swallowed my pride and opened the door, stepping out onto the balcony.

CHAPTER 19

I always hated Halloween. It was a terrible holiday, promoting diabetes and commercialism amongst our children. The real bitch of it was, once you got old enough to start having good costume ideas, suddenly you're too old to trick-or-treat. Your hilarious pumpkin carving idea turns into a smelly fly trap when you're parents aren't around to remember to dispose of it or worse, be the ones to clean it out of your mailbox after some punks stuff it in there as retribution for giving them candy corn. The only redeeming quality about it was the women.

God, the women.

It was the one day of the year that all women actively chose to dress up like sluts. Guys would just half-ass a 'hobo' costume with a ratty sweatshirt or a 'biker' outfit with a leather jacket they found in the closet, but girls, girls really committed to it, and we were more than happy to support them. It was civic obligation. You got the feeling they would dress this way all the time if the biggest cockblock of all – *society* – wasn't there to tell them not to.

That year Anna got the notion to dress up like a slutty Alice from Alice In Wonderland. At least that's what the tag said. I thought it looked more like a slutty

French maid outfit, but hey, who the hell was I to complain?

The funny thing about Anna is that when she wanted to be, she could be the sexiest girl in the room, she just never seemed to 'own' it. Like there was always a voice in the back of her head telling her that it wasn't worth it or she wasn't good enough or something. She dressed in plain clothes for work and plain clothes for school, but when a costume party rolled around she always pulled out all the stops to make herself look like something out of a playboy mag.

I didn't really give a shit about costume parties, and always found them to be a little silly. It seemed like a waste of money and effort to put together an elaborate costume you would wear for one night and probably end up throwing up all over. We had a bit of a row that year about which character from Wonderland I would be to match her. I could even remember a male character from the story until she started listing them off, but after she bullied me out of my indifference, I eventually settled on the Mad Hatter. She got a gigantic top hat and a novelty polka-dot tie from a craft store for me, and bam, I was ready to go.

The night started off fairly well. She drove us over to her friend Dana's house so they could get ready together and do each other's hair. Kevin, Dana's husband, and I watched the World Series on TV, smoked some weed, and made small chat until they finally emerged from the bedroom, as gorgeous as ever. We each took a minute to ogle our respective mates and complement them, and then we seemed ready to go party hopping.

"Wait, we can't go yet," Anna suddenly interjected. "Nick's not here yet."

"Nick...?" I said, sure it couldn't be the same person I was thinking of.

"Hold on, I'll call him."

She dialed some numbers on her phone and stepped into the next room as I remembered a conversation that had taken place earlier that week while we were at dinner.

"Would it make you uncomfortable if Nick came with us to the party?" she had asked.

"Does it matter?" I remarked, contemplatively. "He's your friend, and I'm not going to prevent you from seeing someone for the rest of your life just because I'm jealous."

She narrowed, her eyes, considering, and then began to change the conversation to something else. I nodded and responded generically to the new thread of discussion, but my mind was still on Nick. In truth, no, I wasn't comfortable with her partying with her ex-boyfriend. I was in somewhat of a tight spot, however. Do I admit my insecurities about our relationship and possibly incur her wrath for 'not trusting her'? Or do I let things play out, and run the risk of playing defense all night, worrying at every turn that the old spark between them might be re-ignited? I didn't not want Nick to come, exactly, what I wanted was for her not to want him to come. But she did, so I went along with it.

The night started off fairly well. The first party we went to was in some dude's garage in the suburbs. We played a few rounds of peer bong and I drank my face off, but I couldn't shake this feeling of dread that hovered over the evening. It was a sensation I was familiar with by now, the notion that tonight, something bad was going to happen. That I was going to make a fatal mistake. Sometimes I could sidestep these occurrences by drinking until I passed out, or leaving the party before I met my destiny, but it was always a cowards way out. My anxiety about what would happen tonight, was surely as unfounded as it was every other night, and tonight I would conquer my fears.

I was wrong. That night was a night of destiny, a night of circumstance and calculation. I should have ran, fled into the night. How I wish I had.

Fighting this notion of horrible things to come all night, we at long last arrived back at Dana and Kevin's house. Things had begun to settle down and Anna and I sat together on the couch, cuddling and kissing like we used to, before the honeymoon period of our relationship had left us with all these doubts and nagging insecurity. Suddenly, she leapt from my arms and began racing to the bathroom, her covering her mouth with her palm. It was time to purge.

My eyes caught Dana's as I rose off the couch in pursuit. She narrowed her eyes at me and I gave her a sad glance, as if to say 'this again?'

I rounded the bend and pushed the bathroom door open. Nina's face hovered over the toilet bowl, her whole body shaking with every breath. I knelt down beside her, held her hair up and looked away. I couldn't bear to see her like this, and every time it got harder and harder.

I used to think my aversion was because I didn't like to see her hurting, or in a state of weakness. It didn't jive with my ideal notion of her as a perfect woman. It was then I discovered the affirmation of her humanity wasn't why it made me uncomfortable.

I admit to partying a little too hard every now and then. Sometimes it happens, we over indulge in the things that make us feel good. But she was like this every single time. I used to think I hated going to parties with her because unstructured social interaction made me nervous, but in truth, it was because I knew inevitably, it was going to lead down this road.

She was an alcoholic.

How had I never noticed before? What other empirical truths about her and the world had I blinded myself to because they were inconveniently at odds with my beliefs? What else was she that I couldn't accept?

I didn't feel disgust, like I usually felt when I recognized people had let addiction cause their lives to spiral out of control, instead I felt...angry. I felt betrayed. Why did she do this to herself? To us? Why was she seeking solace in the drink? What was she trying to numb herself to? So many unanswered questions...

Suddenly, she swung her elbow out. I deftly took a step back to avoid a painful strike to the kidney.

She...she tried to hit me.

My eyes went wide with shock as I looked to her for an explanation.

"You're doing it wrong!" she called out, in between heaves.

"W-what?" I replied, meekly.

"You're holding my hair wrong! Oh, for god's sake, I'll do it..." She pulled her own hair back into a pony-tail and resumed her purging.

"I was just trying to help..."

"Yeah, well, you can't take care of me, David. Go get someone else." There was a cruelty in her voice I had never heard before, a venomous bile that shocked and horrified me. Why was she doing this?

Who are you?

"N-no, I want to stay..." I called back, hoping this was just some sort of cruel test of my loyalty.

"Dammit, David!" She turned and looked up at me, with eyes full of fire. "If you can't find someone who'll take care me, I'll get them myself!"

I took a deep breath and stepped out of the bathroom, closing the door behind me. What had I done to deserve this?

"How is she?" Dana whispered as she snuck up to my side.

"She kicked me out. Will you please check on her?"

Dana nodded and opened the door. I stood there for a minute, listening to see if Anna's rage was expressed generally or specifically directed at me, but ultimately decided it didn't matter. It was unfair either way.

I stepped out onto the back porch to have a cigarette and think things over. Horrible realization after horrible realization bubbled to the surface of my mind and I knew I had come to a crossroads. Was I really a loser because I didn't find this sort of lifestyle appealing? I had told myself there was something wrong with me for so long that I had really started to believe it.

I smoked probably half a pack of cigarettes out there, standing in the cold. I didn't want to go back inside. I didn't want to face my life. I was so tired of everything, the endless nights, the countless fights, the yelling, the crying, the worrying, the bowing and scraping and tip-toeing around everything I said and did because I was just so scared of hurting her and driving her away again. She had convinced me for all these years that everything bad that happened to me was my own fault so I lived perpetually in fear of the next train wreck I wasn't smart enough to be able to see coming. *This had to end.*

I stepped back into the house and noticed Anna standing in the kitchen. She was making a sandwich, clearly having puked herself into starvation, and now requiring more sustenance. At least it wasn't more alcohol, I thought. I watched her put that sandwich together lovingly, with care, and was reminded of all the times she had made me sandwiches. They always tasted so good when she made them for some reason.

Even after all this...I still love her.

I decided to swallow my pride and apologize, just like I always did, because I knew I wasn't like her. I didn't need to be 'right' all the time. There were things I was willing to sacrifice for the person I loved. My identity, my pride, my principles — all just word, empty concepts that meant nothing if their application did not produce desirable outcomes.

I took a step forward, and then stopped in my tracks. My ears perked up and isolated her voice amidst the crowd of people. She was talking. She was talking to Nick...about me.

"He just doesn't understand," she said to Nick, who was also watching her prepare her meal He nodded intently. "He just doesn't understand why I feel so *alone*."

My heart sank at her words. She felt lonely? Why didn't she ever tell me?

She tried to. You wouldn't listen. You wouldn't listen because you couldn't accept that she carries the same pain you do.

"He won't open up to me," she said.

Every time I tried to, you would get mad at me. You would throw it in my face. You trained me not to, because you think I'm someone else.

Their conversation continued for a minute, but I couldn't listen to it any longer. I waited a few seconds and walked up to her, grabbing her arm.

"Can we talk?"

"Okay," she said, her voice giving no indication that she was even slightly upset. If I hadn't been eavesdropping, I would never have known the truth, would I?

"Let's go outside."

I lead her out the front door, because I knew this might get ugly. I didn't want everyone to see us argue. Even though they were all complete idiots, burnt-out, alcoholic, drug-addicts who under normal circumstances I would have nothing to do with, I still cared about what they thought. I cared, because she cared.

"Are you still mad at me?" I ventured, after a moment of silence.

"Mad?" she asked curiously, "Why would I be mad at you?" She honestly had no recollection of screaming at me in bathroom, despite the fact it had happened not 15 minutes ago.

I shook my head and looked down at the concrete below. "Nevermind. It's not important."

It's important to me.

"I heard what you said to Nick," I continued, trying to muster all the courage I could to see this through. I told myself that she wasn't going to break up with me for being honest with her. I told myself she loved me as much as I loved her. I told myself we were going to be okay. I told myself so many lies because of her.

"I heard you tell him that you were lonely. I'm sorry..." my voice grew shaky. "I'm so sorry you feel that way."

She shook her head, and sat down on the stoop, exhaling deeply. "It's not your fault, David. We're just two different people... " She wouldn't make eye contact with me as she continued narrating. "We don't have anything in common; we don't like the same things or people... "

Finally, she looked up at me, and asked the most important question of my life. "Why do you even *love* me?"

I scowled at her, hurt by her implication that my feelings for her where not valid or authentic. "Love isn't a choice, Anna! You don't logically choose to fall in love with people, it just happens!"

"That's not—"

She wasn't accepting of my answer, so interrupted her with a new one. "I love that you're smart, I love that you're independent, I love that you're courageous, I love that you're always confident of yourself, I love—"

"I'm not any of those things, David..." She said, looking away. "You don't know me...and I don't know you." Every word she spoke felt like a million tiny needles in my heart. "Maybe... maybe we're both in love with people that don't exist anymore...or maybe never did."

My legs fell out from underneath me and I collapsed onto the cold concrete.

"How... How can you..." I struggled to make a coherent thought, but the despair creeping into my brain had taken hold. There is no way to talk yourself out of this one.

"I... I thought...but you said..." My words grew even more awkward as my vision grew cloudy with tears.

She stood up and looked down at me. Her eyes were full of tears, but she spoke calmly, with a surgical precision. "I wanted you to be the one, David... I wanted it so badly..."

The cruel subtext echoed in my mind: *you are not the one. She doesn't love you. She never did and she never will.*

I stood up slowly and looked into her eyes. Was there anything there? A hint of love? Longing? Desire? Were her words betraying her true feelings?

No. Her eyes were as empty as her stomach. She felt *nothing*.

"Look, we...we don't have to decide anything tonight. We can talk more tomorrow..."

For a moment I thought I might take her up on her offer. I knew what she really meant was that it was over but she didn't want to be alone tonight, but I had convinced myself of so many half-truths over the years, I could easily deceive myself into thinking things were okay for one more night. One last night together. It was romantic, in a way.

"I'm going home." I said as I turned away. "I'm sure Nick can take care of you."

"You're going to walk back...? My place is 10 miles from here!"

"I don't care...I like walking. I need to be somewhere safe tonight. "

I just wanted so badly to get away. It was well below freezing and I was in a bad neighborhood, but I just didn't care, I had to LEAVE. With one last heavy sigh, she pulled her car keys from her purse and placed them in my hand.

"Good night..." she whispered and began walking back towards the house.

"Good bye, Anna."

I entered the car and started the engine. I gave the house, and her, one last glance, as I sat in the driver's seat of my now ex-girlfriend's car. Part of me wanted to drive it off a cliff, part wanted me to set fire to it or wrap it around a telephone pole, and part of me wanted to leave it just as it was, and walk home in the cold.

A dense fog had set in by the time I worked up the nerve to pull out of the driveway. I couldn't see more than 10 feet in front of me, even with the headlights on, but it was early morning, the day after Halloween. I knew there wouldn't be many cars on the road.

Every intersection became a red light, a blockade preventing me from making what would have otherwise been my hasty escape. I'd watch and count the moments until the colored light changed red to green and desperately hope that the next one would not give me time to sit, time for my brain to wander and risk processing the events that had just transpire.

What would I decide when it was all said and done? That this was for the best? That I deserved nothing less? That I had fucked up everything all over again and even though five years had passed I was no wiser or compassionate, no better off as a human being that when I had started this journey? The thought of all the possible permutations that I might land on the coming to terms with my situation filled me with more dread and anxiety than the actual doing of the contemplation itself.

How would I make this okay? What stories would I tell myself to make it all go away? I would I settle for 'she had been unfaithful to me' — a suspicion I had never quite managed to verify — or would I eventually land on a realization that she had been downright abusive? Would I grow to hate her this time? Or would absence once again make the heart grow fonder and hide the truth of it from me? Years later, would I be remembering this night not as it was, but as it might have been: a crossroads where I, despite all odds, chose to stay on the most well-worn path.

Every stone I turned over in my mind bore new questions to replace it, and there was nothing I could decide on for certain. Perhaps there was no way to settle this matter, perhaps there was no lesson to be learned from this painful experience, and I would simply have to go through the subsequent days, weeks, months, years even, hurting the way I always had, but this time without even the recourse to live in the delusional hope of redemption that might come later.

How long would I wait for her this time, I wondered. How long would it be before I chose to live again?

CHAPTER 20

"Anna?" I asked, closing the balcony door behind me, part to keep the chill from entering the house, part to ensure no third-parties would interfere with my plans.

Anna was standing at the balcony railing, staring out across the courtyard. She gave me a half-glance over her shoulder and spoke. "D-David?"

Her voice was shaky, she had clearly been crying. She cleared her throat and fussed with her makeup frantically, trying to cover up her emotional state to no avail. I approached her slowly, giving her time to do whatever she thought she had to do to convince me her answer to my next question was an honest one.

"Are you alright?"

She clenched her teeth and arched her eyebrows, giving me a slight nod before answering. "Yeah. Yeah, I'm fine."

She dusted off the bottom of her ghostly white skirt and sat down on a stone bench in between two potted plants beside the railing.

"Oh, is that for me?" She asked, motioning to the glass in my hand. It wasn't, but I offered it anyway.

"Yeah...here."

I handed the champagne to her and she downed it all in one gulp before throwing the glass over the balcony. A faint echo of glass shattering against concrete bounced off the sides of the house. I sat down next to her on the bench, cautiously.

"What's wrong? Did...Did you and Nick have a fight?"

She grimaced, clearly holding back tears.

"Yes... No. I don't know..." she whispered desperately. "He said...he said he saw the way I was looking at you. I told him he was being jealous over nothing, but...but maybe he was right, David."

She took a few breaths and steadied herself, looking deeply into my eyes. "Maybe I screwed up again... Maybe I made a mistake." I sat in silence. Maybe Tyler's training hadn't prepared me for this. "Do you...do you still think about me?"

"Always." I whispered calmly.

She nodded, looking to the floor. "I've been so cruel to you, David...I'm so sorry. You must hate me..."

"I love you, Anna." I said, mustering some courage from the bowels of my soul. "I always have and I always will." She looked up again, her eyes turning more and more glassy with every word.

This was it. You're doing great, keep going.

"I...sit by the phone every night, waiting for you to call."

Good, beautiful, perfect. You're in the zone. I could feel Tyler's ghost smiling down on me. Anna's lips trembled, and she leaned in, stroking the sides of my face with the back of her hand.

"What would you say if I did...?" I could feel her hot breath on my face, her intoxicating scent penetrating my olfactory. This was it. This was the moment I was waiting for.

"I...I wanted to tell you..."

Say it. Say all those things you ever meant to say. She's yours.

And then...I thought of Nina. Her smiling face, her kindness, her loyalty. What was I doing?

"I wanted to tell you how angry I was with you." I said, a biting harshness dripping from my words.

"W-what...?" She said, clearly shocked at my sudden change in demeanor.

"For the past month, I've been sitting in my apartment, thinking about how to get you back. I've schemed and I plotted and somewhere along the line I asked myself why. Why did I want you back so badly?"

I stood up from the bench, freeing myself from her treacherous grasp. A passionate, indignant air came over me, possessing my body, clawing its way to the surface.

"What did you ever give me besides and inferiority complex and self-esteem issues, Anna? What did you ever give me besides a perpetually moving goal post, a carrot on a stick, a ghost I could chase forever and ever and never actually catch?"

She sat in a stunned silence as I continued my tirade.

"I gave you everything. I gave myself up to you. I spent the past five years of my life trying to change who I was because I thought then, maybe you'd love me. Maybe then I would be deserving of your time and attention. And when you came back to me, I thought, all my effort had finally paid off. All the nights of crying and hating myself and praying and tearing myself to shreds had finally meant something. And this time, I wasn't going to make the same mistakes I did last time. So I went to your parties that I hated, and made friends with the people that disgusted me, and tried to be your little boy toy, the guy with the cool backwards visor and polo shirt that you could drag around and dress up like a cardboard cutout and show off to your friends. But that's not me, Anna. That never was, and that never will be. And I'm done trying to be something that I'm not."

"David, I... I never asked you to change..."

"No, you never asked me to, but you sure as hell didn't try and stop me, did you? You said it yourself; you wanted me to be 'the one'. You wanted me to be something other than me. You took me to those parties. You put me in those places I didn't want to be. You watched me try to be something other than what I am. You watched as I betrayed everything I ever thought was important, turn my back on who I was as a person, for you, and you didn't do a goddamn thing to stop me. You *wanted* me to change. All I ever wanted you to say was that you loved me for who I was, and that I didn't need to change. I'll tell you one thing, Anna," I said, leaning in close, "I may not have been the perfect boyfriend. I may have been jealous and insecure, but I never tried to change you. I loved you. I loved you when you were happy, I loved you when you were sad, I loved you when you were nice, I loved you when you were screaming at me. I loved you when you left me, and I loved you when you came back. I would never have changed a thing."

"David, I—"

"You know what the most fucked up thing was? I would have waited for you, again. I would have lived the rest of my life in fear of the day you'd come back into my life, because I know that no matter where I was or who I was with I would drop everything for another chance to be with you. Because I know, with every fiber of my soul, that we were meant to be together. But I've come to realize you were right about one thing Anna. Love isn't enough. So I'm finally done. I'm not going to spend another 5 years waiting for 'next time' to get it right. I *like* who I am, Anna. I'm not going to hate myself for that anymore. This is goodbye, Anna. For the last time."

I turned away; somewhat concerned my heart would leap out my chest from the massive rush of adrenaline. I heard her sobs as I pulled the balcony door open. In life, many leave, but few look back. Introspection was an activity I freely engaged in whenever the opportunity presented itself, but in this, for the first time in my life, I could not bring myself to look back.

I re-entered the ball room and closed the door behind me, exhaling deeply. *What have I done?*

"There you are!" Nina shouted, rushing up to me. Her heels were slung over her shoulders, and beads of sweet trickled down the sides of her face. Her smile was as bright as ever.

"Where have you been?! I've been looking everywhere for you, it's almost midnight, I—mmmph!"

I wrapped my arms around Nina and pressed my lips against hers. I closed my eyes and held her tightly, never wanting to let go. A perfect moment of clarity struck me as her hands wound around my neck.

"Five!"

The answer had been in front of me the whole time. *I wanted Nina.* This was Tyler's plan. He knew all along that we were perfect for each other, I had just been too obsessed with this misguided notion of self-flagellation and loyalty to notice.

"Four!"

She was perfect for me in every single way. She was the one I had been waiting for all these years, not

Anna. A beam of light illuminated my mind and chased away the murk that had clouded my thoughts all these years. How many people had I left past by me that I might have loved if I hadn't closed myself off to the world? How many opportunities had I let slip by me because I was obsessed, consumed with this notion that without Anna life was not worth living?

"Three!"

Not this time. Never again. This was one opportunity I would seize. I was done living a life full of regrets. I pressed Nina's body against mine, tears beginning to stream down my cheeks. I couldn't remember a time in my life when I was this happy.

"Two!"

I was finally free.

"One! Happy new year!" The crowd burst into raucous hooting and hollering, kazoos blasted and firecrackers popped all around us. I pulled away from Nina and opened my eyes.

"Wow," she said, catching her breath, "That was...amazing." Her eyes had taken on a glass of their own. "What did I do to deserve a kiss like that?"

I glanced over her shoulder towards the balcony. Anna was no longer there. *She was gone.*

"You're you, Nina. You're just *you*. Nothing more and nothing less. I couldn't think of someone more worthy of my affection."

My logical brain was doing the talking, but only because the emotional hemisphere had devolved into intense bliss and baby talk. Somehow, a single, pure though emerged from the storm of feelings that raced through my mind. Everything else quieted for a moment and I breathed life into the thought, gave it form and shaped it, and brought it into the world.

"I love you."

Three small words escaped my lips. They were such a simple thing, but I had never dreamed I might say them again as long as I had lived to any other than she who had been their sole recipient for all these years. Suddenly, it felt as though a weight had been lifted from my shoulders, a burden shared that I no longer need carry alone. A secret I had long harbored within finally shared with a confidant, and the mystique, the tabooness of it, lost in the process.

Nina smiled softly, and pressed her forehead against my chest.

"Oh, David..."

She did not return my sentiment with words, nor did she need to. The reciprocity of the feeling was not prerequisite to its existence or validity. I had found truth in the knowing of it, and in a world where we can know so few things for certain, truth is as valuable as precious gold.

"Excuse me, ladies and gentlemen!" Tyler's voice boomed over the crowd from the speaker system. He had somehow climbed up a gigantic marble statue in the entry way and was sitting on top of the giant marble colossus, a microphone in one hand and a bottle of champagne in the other.

"Thank you all for coming out tonight, and welcome to the new year!" The crowd burst into thunderous applause. "My resolution this year," he paused, taking a swig from the bottle, "is to have even more fun than I did last year!"

More shouts of jubilation from all in attendance. I smiled and raised my drink. "To Tyler!" I bellowed.

"To Tyler!" They replied in unison. Tyler smiled and threw his glasses into the audience. I caught his gaze and mouthed 'thank you' to him. He smiled modestly and nodded.

"Hey, let's get out of here." I said, turning back to Nina.

"And go where?" She replied, arching her eyebrows suspiciously.

"Anywhere."

The limo was waiting for us out front, and the driver smiled kindly as we approached. I held the door open for Nina as she climbed in, and as I looked back at the mansion, I heard a noise. In the side garden, Anna was there, bent over a potted plant, puking her guts out. Nick stood behind her, holding her hair back like I used to. He looked at me, with a pain in his eyes that I recognized. It was the pain I had carried with me for years, and now it was gone.

"Which way are you going, sir?" The driver called through the divider.

I looked at Nina, who had curled up on my lap, laying her head against my shoulder. I ran my thumb down her arm and across her palm, intertwining my fingers with hers.

"Where else? Forward."

"Very good, sir," the driver remarked as he closed the divider, clearly missing the profundity in my realization. Nina and I sat in silence for a few moments, until at last she spoke.

"You know, for a second there I thought that you were just using me to make that Anna girl jealous."

I pulled her face towards mine with the crook of my finger.

"Now, why would I do a thing like that?"

She smiled, kissing my fingertip. "My mistake." A mischievous look came over her face and she suddenly pulled me down onto the floor of the limo.

"Ever done it in a limo?" she whispered, her hot breath tickling my ear.

"Once," I joked, "but it didn't go very well."

She smiled and began pulling the buttons off my shirt. Her hair glimmered in the moonlight as she looked down at me. My heart-pitter pattered and butterflies laid nervous eggs in my stomach. *I felt so alive.* Time had finally begun to start again for me in that limousine, the hour hand on my internal clock finally wrested free from the position it had been stuck in for so long. *I was 15 again.*

No thoughts of Anna entered my mind as I considered my happiness. For the first time in years I did not hear her voice in my head when I closed my eyes. No longer did I long for her affection and approval, that I might finally be the man I dreamed to be.

Nina pulled my shirt open and bent down, hovering her lips a few scant inches above mine.

"Everyone makes mistakes."

Made in the USA
Lexington, KY
06 February 2010